Penguin Books

Good-night, Prof, Love

Graham Hollis is nearly seventeen. If he can pass his exams and join his father's accountancy firm he'll live happily ever after – anyway, that's how his parents see it. Graham sees things a bit differently. He's bored with life in Crimley (hardly the most exciting place on earth) and he fantasizes about the wonderful, glamorous girl who's going to bring romance and excitement into his life. But the girl who's going to create the first spark of real love in Graham Hollis is in fact short, rather stumpy and works in Jeff's Café as a waitress. Graham can't believe he's falling for her but he is, and she's about to give him the adventure of a lifetime . . .

John Rowe Townsend is an acclaimed writer for young people and *Good-night, Prof, Love* is one of his best books for teenagers. His other books in Plus include *Noah's Castle*, *A Foreign Affair*, *The Intruder* and *Cloudy/Bright*. John Rowe Townsend now lives in Cambridgeshire.

John Rowe Townsend

Good-night, Prof, Love

Penguin Books

PENGUIN BOOKS

Published by the Penguin Group
27 Wrights Lane, London w8 5tz, England
Viking Penguin Inc., 40 West 23rd Street, New York, New York 10010, USA
Penguin Books Australia Ltd, Ringwood, Victoria, Australia
Penguin Books Canada Ltd, 2801 John Street, Markham, Ontario, Canada l3r 1b4
Penguin Books (NZ) Ltd, 182–190 Wairau Road, Auckland 10, New Zealand

Penguin Books Ltd, Registered Offices: Harmondsworth, Middlesex, England

First published by Oxford University Press 1970
Published in Peacock Books 1977
Reprinted with slight revisions in Penguin Books 1989
10 9 8 7 6 5 4 3 2 1

Typeset, printed and bound in Great Britain by
Hazell Watson & Viney Limited
Member of BPCC Limited
Aylesbury, Bucks, England
Set in Linotron 202 Bembo

Chapter One

. . . He was walking on cliffs, somewhere on the south coast, somewhere remote and beautiful. White chalky cliffs where the green downs came to a stop. It was a clear blue day, the seagulls wheeling and dipping. Nobody was in sight. The cry for help floated up from far below. He stepped to the edge, looked down over the dizzying drop. She was lying there on a perilously narrow ledge. She was obviously hurt . . .

'And mind you have proper meals,' his mother said.

'Yes.'

'And don't stay indoors all day. Get a bit of exercise.'

'Yes.'

'But wrap yourself up well if you go out in the evenings. They get chilly, these September nights.'

'Yes.'

'And don't let any strangers into the house.'

'Yes. I mean no.'

'You're not listening. You never listen.'

'I *am* listening.'

The boy was tall, very tall, and thin. The boy was not quite seventeen. He was fair and wore spectacles. The boy's name was Graham Hollis. He lived with his parents in a town called Crimley in the industrial North Midlands. Between interruptions the boy was day-dreaming.

. . . He was walking on cliffs, somewhere on the

south coast, somewhere remote and beautiful. From far below, the cry floated up to him. She was lying on a ledge, her leg bent strangely under her. Farther down, the sea broke cruelly on the rocks. Graham didn't hesitate. He let himself down over the edge, scrambling, feeling for handholds. He was there beside her. She was slender, her face pale, her hair long and dark. She was conscious, was able to whisper, 'You shouldn't have risked it.' He slid an arm under her shoulders . . .

'I still think he should be coming with us,' his mother said to his father.

'I keep telling you I'll be all right,' Graham said.

'Most boys of your age would jump at the chance of a week's touring in Ireland before the school term starts.'

'You know I'm always car-sick.'

'You're not car-sick if it's somewhere you want to go.'

'Too late now, anyway,' Mr Hollis said. 'Lilian, if you'll just pour me another cup of tea, I'll be bringing the suitcases downstairs while it cools.'

. . . 'Are you much hurt?' Graham asked the girl. She smiled, bravely. 'It's my ankle,' she whispered. 'Only a sprain, I think . . .'

'And if you were determined not to go to Ireland,' Mrs Hollis said to Graham, 'you could have spent the week with your Uncle Roger and Aunt Josie at Pool-on-Sea. We could have delivered you there and picked you up afterwards. But no, you won't do anything sensible. You have to stay here, all on your own. It just doesn't seem natural at your age.'

'Think of all the studying I'll get done,' Graham said.

'It's possible to work too hard.'

6

'I need to pass the exam next June. As Dad keeps reminding me.'

'I know,' said Mrs Hollis. 'But at sixteen you should be having a good time and *doing* things, like the other boys. I sometimes wonder if you're quite normal.'

'I'm normal all right,' Graham said.

'I must admit, I wouldn't be so keen on leaving you alone in the house if you were in one of those party-giving sets. I hear of such things going on these days I can hardly believe it. I haven't that to worry about, anyway. At least, I should hope not. You will behave yourself, won't you, and not do anything silly?'

'One minute you wish I was having a good time,' said Graham. 'Next minute you're afraid I'll be having wild parties all over the house. Make up your mind what you're supposed to be worrying about.'

'I'm not happy about leaving you, that's the long and short of it,' Mrs Hollis said. 'If it wasn't for your father, forever saying it's all right –'

'Come on, now!' Mr Hollis called from the doorway. 'Graham, you can help load the car. Put the two big suitcases in the boot, will you? Lilian, what became of the blue holdall? And my toilet-bag and electric shaver?'

'You can't have looked for them,' Mrs Hollis said. 'They're all there in the bathroom. I wouldn't have thought even *you* could miss them. I don't know what you'd do without me.'

Mr Hollis winked at Graham.

Graham walked out with a suitcase in each hand and stowed them in the car. In the wide Victorian avenue the trees were yellow, the leaves starting to fall. Mrs Hollis came down the drive, carrying her bag.

7

'Go round last thing at night,' she said. 'Make sure the doors are locked. And the downstairs windows fastened. And the gas turned off. And no taps running.'

'Yes,' said Graham. 'Yes, Mother. Yes. Yes.'

'And don't be eating fried food all the time. You know your stomach's your weak point. And remember to write to us at the address I gave you in Connemara. And post the letter by Monday or we shan't get it.'

'Yes.'

Mr Hollis got into the driver's seat of the dark blue Rover. He lowered the window and shook Graham's hand.

'Look after yourself, young man,' he said. He winked again. 'And be good.'

The car drew away. Graham waved. Twenty yards along the street it stopped. His mother leaned out.

'Don't forget to change your underclothes!' she called.

– Gone. Peace at last. Street empty now. A fine day but looking like autumn. Moist and hazy, sun coming through, but barely over the roof-tops.

– Go back into the house. Silent, deserted. You can hear your own footfall, hear the clock tick, feel sad for a moment. But a pleasant sadness. A parent-less week. Long quiet hours, freedom, eat what you like when you like.

– If you got bored you could ask John Wyatt round. Concoct a meal together, with frying-pan and row of cans. Print up a few photographs, talk about old Stebbings and the holiday maths assignment. You could, but you don't have to. Something appealing

8

about slight loneliness, even slight boredom. And John Wyatt's not the company you want, not really.

. . . He'd dragged her to safety, up a narrow sheep-track. She lay now in sunshine on top of the cliff. He'd folded his jacket to make a pillow for her. 'I'll go for help,' he told her. 'You can't get far with that ankle.' But she put out a hand to touch his. 'Not just yet,' she said. 'Don't leave me.'

. . . Perhaps he hadn't actually rescued her. Perhaps he'd just met her on the cliffs, wandering, as solitary as himself. They'd hardly spoken, but they'd understood each other, they were kindred spirits. Now she was running ahead of him, barefoot, calling, 'You can't catch me.' She was running down a tiny, winding path into the next cove, running across the sands . . .

– Now then, Graham. Get a grip. No more of that nonsense.

– No harm in it.

– No good in it either. Dreaming. That's what brings comments. Remember old Stebbings: 'I see that Hollis has withdrawn to his desert island again.' And Father: 'Are you in a daze, lad? Do you know you passed Mrs Grimshaw in the High Street today and looked right through her?' And Mother: 'Three hours on that problem and you haven't finished it yet. Why can't you get your homework done in reasonable time, like everyone else?'

– Dreaming. You ought to write a book on it. *How to Waste Time*, by Graham Hollis.

– All right, all right, we know what it's all about. We know what's missing in your life. We know what you need. A girl. And what's the problem? Easy enough to get fixed up. You only have to go where the young people go. Where Ken Harper goes, and John Wyatt, and Beth Edwards across the street. Go

9

to the beat club, or even the crummy youth group in the church hall. Soon get paired off. Easy.

– Paired off after a fashion. But who wants pairing off with such as Beth Edwards? Beth Edwards, essence of suburban Crimley. Stepping out, Crimley style, twenty years behind the times. Cinema Thursday, youth club Friday, tennis on Saturday, church on Sunday, that was the end of Solomon Grundy. You can keep Beth Edwards. And all like her.

. . . The girl was slim, her face pale, her hair long and dark. She wasn't like any girl ever seen in Crimley. She was running ahead of him, barefoot, calling, 'You can't catch me.' Running down a winding path into the next cove, running into the sea, splashing through shallow water . . .

– Come off it, boy. Write out five hundred times, I must not rescue imaginary damsels in distress. I must not rescue imaginary damsels. I must not rescue imaginary. I must not rescue. I must not. I must. I.

– How about a cup of tea, then getting on with that maths problem?

– What, a cup of tea already, half an hour after breakfast?

– Why not? No one for a whole week to tell you what not to do. Enjoy it, Graham boy. A cup of tea every half hour all day long if you like. The hours, the quiet free hours. Do as you will.

. . . They were running hand in hand now, parallel with the shore, splashing through shallow water. Like a scene from a film . . .

– Oh no. Not again. Put that kettle on.

– Get some exercise, Mother said. She would. Still, it's a good idea after a lunch like that. Bacon, fried egg, sausages, fried bread, baked beans, fried tomatoes. A feast. Maybe enough would have been as good as.

– You dozed.

– I never.

– You dozed. Woke up, mouth stale, no work done. Get some exercise.

– A walk, that's the thing. Put shoes on, check you've locked all doors, keys in pocket. Set off uphill towards the moors. Pity about old Sport. He loved a walk. You only had to say it – 'Walk, Sport!' – and he'd be on the alert, jumping up at you, slapping the floor with his tail. Even 'Shops!' would rouse him. Poor old Sport. Must be a year since he died. We ought to have had another. Sport the Second. Wouldn't have been the same, though.

– Half-way up the hill already. Gill's seat. Sounds rude. Presented to the town by Alderman Gill. In memory of whatever it was. The vantage-point. Quite a view, you have to admit it. Sit down, boy, take a look. Not for the first time. Crimley. Smoke, railway, dirty river, chimneys. Town centre in hollow, hills all round, sloping suburbs. Crimley.

– You're here for life, boy.

– Oh no.

– Oh yes.

– God forbid.

– God won't. It's all mapped out. Pass the exam next year, go into Father's office. Pass more exams, become qualified, then junior partner. Hollis and Son, accountants. 'And Son.' It was that from the day Dad started the practice. The son was in rompers then. You.

– Hollis and Son, small town accountants. For ever more. Accountants don't move. Where your practice is, there shall your heart be also. In Crimley. Ugly

11

industrial Crimley. Nineteen thousand people, all stuck firmly in the mud. Crimley, the dump.

– What's wrong with Crimley?

– Everything's wrong with Crimley.

– Crimley's all right. Plenty of places worse. Lots of character, all up-and-down, moors on your doorstep.

– Crimley, dead-and-alive. Crimley, one cinema, one bingo hall, a handful of clubs, nothing to do on Sunday.

– Crimley, a great little town.

– Crimley.

– You've seen enough of it for now. Get on with that walk. Farther up the hill, turn right at footpath, along edge of moors, down by parallel road.

. . . And so the days passed, in the south coast village a long way from ugly old Crimley. A swim each morning. Sailing on the bay sometimes. She could handle a boat all right, bare arm brown on the tiller, slim body alert to dart under the boom. In the evenings they'd dance. Or they might take a twilight walk along the cliffs where they'd first met, stopping at times to embrace. Her name was – what was her name? – her name was Barbara. 'I've been so happy with you,' she said when the holiday was over and they had to part. 'We *must* meet again.'

. . . Of course, she could have an aunt in Crimley. 'Crimley?' she said when he told her where he lived. 'Why, yes, of course, my Aunt Susan lives there. She's been wanting me to visit her for years, but I always wondered what I'd do in Crimley, not knowing anyone. But now that I know *you* . . .'

– Come off it, boy, you can't bring her to Crimley. Come off it altogether. Pack her in, she doesn't exist. Get back to real life. Down the hill and home. A week by yourself, a week of peace, nobody to tell you off, no need to make the bed. You can get some of that work done, fry up three times a day if you feel like it. A feast. Though maybe enough is as good as.

— Seems years since they went. Twelve hours in fact. Silence good but gets oppressive. Radio cheerful at first, soon palls. Top tunes third time round are a bore. Television, yes. Feels odd watching it all by yourself, though. Nobody to make comments to, no argument, no irritation, dull. Summer schedules still running. All those repeats. Dead loss. Might phone John Wyatt after all.

'Hullo, Mrs Wyatt, is John in? Oh, I see. Yes, of course, I'd forgotten, Saturday night. Yes, everybody's out Saturday night. Yes, tell him I rang. Tell him it was Graham. Graham Hollis. Hollis. Thank you, Mrs Wyatt. 'Bye.'

— Everyone's out on Saturday night. Everyone but me.

— Well, what's new about that? How often do you go out on Saturday night? Never. Well, hardly ever. But the parents are usually in. It's company. Parents? You're coming up to seventeen, Graham lad. Time you weren't tied to their apron-strings.

— Anyway, there's plenty of that maths to do.

— Oh, to hell with the maths.

— You could fry up again.

— Funny how one big fry-up seems to last all day.

— Have to go out. Not up the hill again. Along the High Street. Where the lights are. Such as they are.

— Coat on. Starting to get chilly in evenings. Remember what Mother said.

— Remember what Mother said? Do you *have* to do what Mother says?

— It does get chilly here, all the same. Check keys.

13

Don't want to have to climb in, specially at night. Somebody might call the police . . . 'But, constable, I live here. My parents are away, they left me behind. But it's true, I'm telling you, it's true. You're not arresting me, constable, are you?' . . .

– Don't be so daft. They wouldn't do anything of the sort.

– Along to the main road, down the hill into Crimley High Street. A few spots of rain on the wind. Past the furniture store, past Woolworths, past Marks & Spencer's. Plenty of people still around. Shop-window gazers. Boys and girls arm in arm.

. . . She slipped her arm into his. 'I'm glad I came to stay with Aunt Susan,' she said. 'It's such fun being here with you.' Her voice was soft and musi-cal, with none of the Crimley harshness. She looked up into his face. They were happy, the two of them together, letting the world go by . . .

'Sorry.'

'Look where you're going, can't you?'

'I'm sorry, I didn't mean to do that.'

– Get a grip, boy, get a grip.

– Head post office, men's outfitters, jewellers, supermarket. Rialto Cinema. Queuing for seats at £2. *The Thing from Under the Earth*. Let's have a look at the stills. Gruesome object. Even *that* seems to have a girl. She doesn't look too pleased about it, though. Maybe I'm better-looking than the Thing from Under the Earth. Just.

– Getting past the centre now. Butcher's, confec-tioner's, newsagent's, laundrette. Jeff's Café. Scruffy joint, Jeff's. Sort of place your parents don't like you to go in. Who'd want to go in Jeff's anyway? Well, there's a question. Not doing much business just now. Truck-drivers' and workmen's place, mainly, and they're not around much on Saturday night.

People having a night out go to the Silver Tree, not Jeff's.

– You could have a meat pie and a cup of tea. In Jeff's, disliked by parents.

– What, pay good money for a pie and a cup of tea when you can have what you like at home for nothing? Don't be daft.

– But that table in the window's empty. You could sit there and watch the world go by. Such as it is. The world of Crimley. As seen from Jeff's Café, disliked by parents.

– Prices painted in white on glass panel of door. Tea 25p, meat pie 50p. That's cheap enough, anyway. Probably horrible. Unhygienic. But to hell with it. It's your ritzy night out. In Jeff's Café, disliked by parents.

– In you go.

. . . You wouldn't bring *her* to a place like this.

Chapter Two

The boy came into the café. No one took any notice of him. He found a seat at the empty table in the window. Most of the other dozen tables were empty, too. Empty of people, anyway. They were littered with cigarette ash, used cups and saucers, plates with remnants of meals.

At the plastic-topped counter a girl was chatting with a customer. A second customer operated a fruit machine. Three more were arguing about racehorses at the table farthest from the door. They and the boy were the only people in the café.

The girl behind the counter recoiled in pretended shock at some remark. She was blonde, round-faced, wearing a white overall, not very white.

'Lynn!' came a man's voice from somewhere out of sight at the back. 'If you've nothing else to do, you could clear some of them dishes away.'

The girl pulled a face, mouthed something in the direction of the voice.

'That's right, you tell him where to go,' said the man at the counter. 'Give the job up, duck. Come out on the town with me.'

'You going to pay my wages?' the girl asked.

'Wages? I don't pay girls to come out with me,' the man said. 'They do it for fun.'

'Find someone who thinks it'd be fun, then,' the girl said.

'Lynn!' called the voice from behind the scenes.

'I'm serving a customer!' she answered.

She looked over in Graham's direction.

'Come up here if you want anything,' she said. 'I don't wait on you. This isn't the Ritz.'

Graham went to the counter.

'A cup of tea and a meat pie, please,' he said.

The tea was stewing in a huge metal pot on a gas ring at the girl's left hand. Pies and sandwiches sat under a glass dome on her right.

'A cup of tea and a meat pie, please,' echoed the man she'd been talking to, in tones of grotesque refinement.

The girl groped under the counter for a plate.

'Miss, miss, hurry, please do!' the man said. 'The young gentleman requires nourishment, urgently.'

'Aw, leave him alone,' the girl said. 'He's all right, aren't you, duck? He's a customer, Sam Bell, same as you are.'

She poured tea into an enormous cup and pushed it across to Graham with a bowl of sugar, brown where the damp spoon had stood in it. She chose a pie with some care.

'Will that do for you, love?' she asked.

The three men at the back table were leaving. One of them dug Sam Bell in the ribs as he went past.

'Hear that, Sam?' he said. 'First "duck", then "love". The lad's cutting you out. You're losing your sweetheart.'

'Get lost,' Sam said. He was big, heavy, narrow-eyed. He didn't seem amused.

'Now, Sam,' the girl said. 'Don't look like that. You know I'm wild about you. It was just seeing the lad that turned my head for a minute. That lovely fair hair and them smashing specs, I couldn't resist them . . . Seventy-five pence, love.'

Graham paid. His face was red.

'I'm getting nowhere tonight,' said Sam. He drained his cup and headed for the door.

'Nor any other night,' Lynn called after him.

Graham picked up his cup and plate and withdrew to his seat in the window.

'Got any more tenpennies, Lynn?' asked the man at the fruit machine.

'No more in the till, mate. You've had 'em all. Jeff might have change.'

'What sort of mood's he in?'

'Not so good, mate.'

'Oh, never mind. Time I was going, anyway. 'Night, Lynn.'

' 'Night.'

Only the girl and Graham were left in the café. The girl took a coin from the till and put it in the juke-box. The tune she chose was one that Graham had heard three times on the radio that day. She did a few steps on her own, sang a few words, not too tunefully. She winked at Graham.

– Attractive, maybe. In a way. Eyes wide-set, mouth generous. Figure all right, legs not bad but a shade too thick. Might be seventeen, more likely eighteen.

– Your mother wouldn't like her.

– So what? Mother doesn't like anything that's young and girl-shaped. Except Beth Edwards, and she's just young.

– Attractive, maybe. In a way. Good-natured-looking. Not your type, though. Mothers apart, not your type. Definitely not.

'Lynn!' The voice from the back. 'What about them dishes?'

'In a minute, Jeff. In a minute.'

She came over to Graham's table, pushed some dirty cups aside, sat on the edge of it.

'Hi, kid,' she said.

Graham blushed, didn't say anything.

'You don't want to take no notice of Sam,' she said. 'Nor any of 'em, when they get like that. They don't mean any harm. It's just their way.'

'Oh, I wasn't bothering,' he said. 'Anyway, it was nice of you to stick up for me.'

'That's nothing. I can hold my own with that lot any day. *You're* not used to it. What you doing here, anyway? I've not seen you before.'

'Oh, I – just dropped in.'

'You a student or something?'

'No, I'm still at school. Here in Crimley. The Royal Grammar School.'

'You must be clever, to have got in there.'

'Not all that clever. I find it hard, keeping up. But my dad pushes me. You know what parents are.'

'No, I don't. Not in that way. The only place my old man ever pushed me was out.'

'You don't live at home, then?'

'Not likely. My home's in Birmingham. If you can call it that.'

'So you live in lodgings here?'

'Sort of.'

She took out cigarettes, offered them to Graham, who refused. She lit one for herself.

'*I* think you look clever,' she said. 'And nothing wrong with it, either. Fellows like Sam Bell, they're jealous, that's the long and short of it. That's why they try and take the mickey. But I told you, don't bother about them, don't take no notice. You only play their game if you do.'

A man came through the green baize curtain that divided the café from the kitchen behind. A man in his middle or late thirties. A man of medium height, broad in shoulders and chest, tapering lower down. A boxer's figure. Face sallow, hair thick and dark, eyes sharp. A formidable man, tough and strong. Obviously the boss. Jeff.

The girl was still sitting on the edge of Graham's table. She drew on her cigarette, blew smoke out unhurriedly.

'Get them dishes cleared and washed up!' the man said.

'It's not my job. You pay me to serve. Clearing up and washing dishes, that's Arthur's job.'

'It's your job tonight, with Arthur off sick.'

'What's wrong with doing it yourself?'

'Oh, nothing, nothing.' The man's tone was sarcastic. 'I pay you to sit around chatting up the customers while I do the work. Is that the idea?'

He looked sharply at Graham.

'You want anything more, lad?'

'No, thank you.'

'Well, if you've finished you can go. It's not a public lounge.'

He turned back to the girl.

'Are you going to get on with it or aren't you?'

'All right, all right, Jeff. Keep calm.'

She got down from the table, still not hurrying. Watched by Jeff she fetched a tray from the counter and began putting dishes on it, slowly, slowly.

– You ought to stick up for her, Graham boy. She stuck up for you a few minutes ago.

– Don't be silly. He's the boss. She has to do as he tells her. Naturally.

– There's more to it than that. Something in the air between them. Thundery, as if a storm could break. If she keeps on going slow.

'Maybe I could help?' he offered on impulse.

'Maybe you could mind your own business,' said Jeff.

'The lad's done you no harm,' Lynn said. 'You

20

don't have to talk to him like that. He's at the Royal Grammar School, if you want to know.'

'What's that got to do with it?'

'You could treat him more polite, that's what.'

Jeff stopped, thought for a minute, then said to Graham:

'I don't care who you are or where you go to school. But you can help if you really want to. We'll have a rush in ten minutes' time, when the pubs close. It's worth a free meal to you. How long can you stay?'

'I can stay till whenever I want,' said Graham.

'Oooh, you old stop-out!' the girl said.

Graham reddened again.

'There, there. Sorry, pet,' she said. 'You see, Jeff, he's sensitive. Be nice to him, like I told you.'

Jeff took no notice of this.

'We close at midnight,' he said. 'Can you stay till then?'

Graham nodded.

'It's worth a fiver to you,' Jeff said. 'But you work for it. Understand?'

Graham nodded again.

'Right. Start now. Take all this stuff to the kitchen sink, behind the curtain there. Wash it, dry it, shove it in the racks. Alice'll show you.'

A bell jangled, the door from the street swung open. Half a dozen men entered, all in a bunch.

'Here they come,' Jeff said. 'First of the many. Hang your coat up. Not here, you don't know what might happen to it. In the kitchen. Then get on with the job.'

Beside the kitchen sink was a stove, and at the stove was Alice, small and thin, in late middle age. Her job was to make toast, grill hamburgers, fry bacon, eggs and chips. She was deft, expressionless, silent.

Graham put on an apron.

– What would *she* say? Your mother. She wouldn't like it. No doubt about that. Working in Jeff's Café. Of all places.

– Why always 'What would Mother say?' She won't know. News won't get to the West of Ireland. Do as you like all week. Free.

– Five pounds. First you've ever earned. Never even had a newspaper-round. A sheltered life. Too sheltered by half.

– No time to think about it anyway. Place filling up quickly. Clear tables, start washing cups and plates, Lynn shouting for more. Half-dry a few, rush them through to her, get on with the rest. Jeff now, wanting tables cleared again. Hurry round with the tray, careful, careful, nearly dropped that lot. Get busy washing, drying. Lynn still wanting clean cups. Can't keep up, can't keep up. Thank God for Alice, she's quick, helping without a word, washing dishes and frying eggs at the same time.

– Frying. Fried food all day, seen, smelled, eaten. Makes your stomach queasy. Never want anything fried again. In café in front, air full of smoke, makes eyes smart. Get used to it, though. Lynn at counter not bothered, coping with all comers, laughing at jokes, bringing customers on. Or holding them off. Handing out orders, quick, accurate.

– Head starting to spin. Can't keep on much longer at this rate.

– Pressure easing off a bit, though. Not so many coming in now.

– What a job. It's hell.

– But fun, in a hellish way. Earning money. First you've ever earned. What would Mother say? Who cares?

Jeff strode through the café, turned the OPEN card on the door to CLOSED, cleared out the lingerers.

'We'll get cleaned up now,' he said.

Graham washed the last cups and plates, and swept litter from the café floor. Alice and Lynn wiped down the kitchen. Jeff was at the till, counting takings. They tipped the stewed liquid from the big teapot down the sink and made fresh tea for themselves. Jeff took a pack of cigarettes from the counter, handed it round, then put it in his pocket. Graham smoked with the rest, suppressing a cough.

Jeff handed him a five-pound note. He slipped it casually into his pocket.

'Old Arthur'll be away for a week,' Jeff said. 'You can come in every night if you like. You'll have to speed up a bit, though.'

'He did fine,' said Lynn. 'Much quicker than Arthur.'

'He couldn't be slower than Arthur. Time old Arthur packed it in. I don't know what I employ him for. Too soft-hearted, that's what's wrong with me.'

'You? Soft-hearted? Like hell you are!' said Lynn.

'Well, do you want to come in for a week, lad?' Jeff asked. 'Please yourself. It's up to you.'

'I don't know,' said Graham.

'Oh, come on, duck,' said Lynn. 'Come in for *me*. I've took quite a fancy to you.' Then, to Jeff: 'You'll have to pay him properly. A tenner a night, that's fair. And cheaper than Arthur, even then.'

'Too much,' said Jeff.

'Go on, you can afford it. You're rolling in the stuff.'

'You keep out of it, Lynn,' said Jeff. 'All right, lad. A tenner a night, from eight to twelve-thirty, tomorrow till next Friday. Take it or leave it. Yes or no?'

'He says yes,' said Lynn.

Graham hadn't said anything. But he nodded, hesitantly.

'Right,' Jeff said. 'What's your name? Graham? Graham what?'

'Hollis.'

'I shall call you Prof,' said Lynn. 'Because you look like a professor. Absent-minded. And them specs. But you're nice, Prof. He's nice, isn't he, Alice? I could fall for him, I reckon.'

'If you're trying to make Jeff jealous,' said Alice, 'you might as well save your breath.'

'Jeff?' said Lynn. 'What's Jeff to me?'

Alice snorted.

'There. Time you was on your way, Prof,' said Lynn. 'Your mum'll be wondering what you're up to, coming in at this time.'

'My parents are away all week,' Graham said.

He got up, swayed a moment, recovered.

'You're looking white, love,' Lynn said.

'I'm all right.'

'Shall I see you home, Prof? Or don't you trust me? Don't worry, I won't come in. Unless I'm asked.'

'Pack it in, Lynn!' said Jeff. His voice was sharp. 'Off you go, Graham. See you at eight o'clock.'

'Good-night, Prof, love,' said Lynn.

Alice looked into the middle distance and said nothing.

' 'Night,' said Graham. He went out into the empty High Street.

– Yes, it's cold.

– As Mother said.

– Still, you're well wrapped up.

– As Mother said.

– Feeling a bit queasy. All those food smells. The cigarette. The bustle. A touch of shock, maybe.

– You've got a job.

– *That's* not as Mother said.

– A job for a week. At Jeff's Café.

– Absurd. Incredible.

– Fact. At Jeff's Café, disliked by parents.

He headed for home.

Chapter Three

Graham got home just in time to be sick. He was sick
again three times during the night. Towards dawn
he fell deeply asleep and woke at midday, weak and
dizzy. He ate a little bread and butter and drank a
glass of milk. It was a fine September Sunday. He sat
in the garden in a deckchair, with a textbook open
on his knee.

. . . Slender, dark and graceful, she came round
the side of the house towards him. Barbara. 'Hullo,
lazybones,' she said. 'Come up on the moors for a
walk. Just the two of us, among the sheep and the
heather. I've walked over from Aunt Susan's
already.' Then she saw that he wasn't well. Her face
was compassionate. 'Oh, you poor thing,' she said.
'You poor, poor thing. There, let me get a chair and
sit with you.' She stroked his forehead with a cool,
dry palm, smiling at him in silent sympathy. 'Barbara,' he said, 'I have a problem. I wonder if you can
help me solve it . . .'

– Stow it, boy. Learn to tell fact from fiction. The
problem's real. She isn't. You were a proper Charlie,
weren't you, saying you'd work at that café all week?
The place that made you feel like this. The noise, the
bustle, the food-smells. You'd better find a way to
get out of it.

– I'm not well enough to go tonight. Isn't that
sufficient excuse?

– Nonsense, you're better already. You kept that
bread and milk down, didn't you? Nothing wrong

26

with you now. Don't chicken out of it. Make up your mind about the whole week. If you don't decide today, you'll have the same problem tomorrow.

– I'd better keep my promise.

– You've broken plenty in your time. Keep it if it's the best thing. Otherwise don't.

– Father always says in his profession a man's word is his bond. People must know they can trust you.

– Father again. It's your decision, not his.

– I think I ought to go.

– That awful place. That awful nasty-eyed ex-boxer. That awful sour, skinny Alice. And that awful girl. Above all, that awful girl.

– She's not so bad.

– Made eyes at you one minute, laughed at you the next.

– But she stuck up for me.

– Only for fun. You know what your mother would call her?

– No, and I don't care.

– Common. That's the word. Common.

– I don't think in those terms.

– You do. You only say you don't. Common.

– She seemed all right in some ways. Not that I'm interested.

– Common. And her legs are too thick.

– Don't forget they're paying me. A tenner a night. Two weeks' pocket-money every night.

– So what? You're not short, are you?

– It's nice having money. Puts you on a level with people who've left school.

– You're side-tracking. You don't care about the money. You know you don't. You've five hundred pounds in the bank. Plenty. It's a matter of people, not money.

– What'll they say if I don't turn up?

– Doesn't matter, does it? They haven't your address.

– I wouldn't like to fall foul of Jeff.

– You won't see him again. He wouldn't do anything, anyway. It's not the end of the world if somebody doesn't turn up for a bit of part-time work. Don't go, boy.

– I might not. And again I might.

– You're thinking of the girl.

– I'm not.

– Forget her. Not your type.

– I never thought she *was*.

– Common. Her legs are too thick.

– Perhaps I won't go.

– That's better.

– Perhaps I will.

He walked slowly along the High Street, at the opposite side from Jeff's. He looked across at it. A dingy establishment, with dark green paintwork starting to peel. It was eight o'clock, beginning to be twilight.

. . . A fine, mild September evening. 'I'm getting quite to like this little town,' she said. 'So long as I'm with somebody nice. Like you. Why don't we stroll along towards the river and lean over the bridge and look down at the water. And look up at the stars.' And so they sauntered off along the High Street, happy in each other's company. Barbara took his arm, looked up into his face . . .

– For heaven's sake, come back to earth. Are you going into Jeff's tonight or not?

– A promise is a promise.

– That awful place. Your parents wouldn't like it. You know they wouldn't.

– What's it to do with them? I'm free.

28

– That awful girl.
– She stuck up for me, didn't she?
– That awful girl.

Graham crossed the road and pushed open the café door.

They were fairly busy. Jeff slung an apron at him. There was a pile of crockery to wash. He washed it, dried it, returned it to the counter. Lynn smiled absently, went on serving and chatting to customers. Graham cleared the tables, washed dishes again. Alice was silent at the stove. Jeff sat in the tiny cubbyhole he used as some kind of office. Then he got up, put on his jacket, said, 'Back in ten minutes.'

Alice, still silent, slapped two eggs and a big portion of bacon on a plate and handed it to Graham. He found he was hungry, and ate. Lynn ate a chocolate biscuit, one of the expensive kind. She winked at Graham.

'Hi, Prof,' she said. 'How you doing?'

'Not so bad.'

'Coping all right tonight, aren't you? Got your skates on.'

'I'm learning.'

Then she was serving a customer again, chatting, answering back, fending off a too-personal remark.

Graham went on clearing tables, washing dishes, drying them, stacking them, putting them back behind the counter, clearing tables, washing dishes, drying them . . . Customers came and went. Jeff returned.

Time passed quickly. It was midnight.

Jeff turned the notice to CLOSED. They cleaned up, made themselves a pot of tea, smoked.

– She hasn't had much to say tonight. Seems to be

thinking of something else. Hasn't made eyes at me, unless you count that wink. Hasn't even teased me.

– Do you want her to?

– No. Just a bit puzzled, that's all. Last night she was nearly begging me to stay. If it wasn't for that, I wouldn't be here now.

– You didn't have to come. Better if you hadn't. Not worth it for a tenner a night.

– Maybe she wasn't interested after all. Just putting on an act for Jeff.

– Could be. Why should she be interested in *you*? You flatter yourself, boy.

– But she *seemed* interested.

– You don't want her to be. That awful girl.

– She stood up for me last night.

– That awful girl.

Jeff took money from the till and paid him. There were some ham rolls and potted-meat sandwiches left over under one of the glass domes. Lynn and Alice didn't want them. Jeff gave them to Graham to take home.

Monday.

A ring at the doorbell.

He staggered downstairs, tousled and dressing-gowned. It was the milkman, waiting to be paid.

'Your mum's away?' the milkman said.

Graham nodded.

'Having a good time?'

'Oh, all right.'

'Just got up, haven't you? Musta been out late last night. Out on the tiles, eh?'

'No,' said Graham, handing over a note and waiting for the change.

'If I was your mum I wouldn't trust you,' the milkman said. He was teasing. 'Why, you might be up to anything. And probably are.' He cupped an ear with his hand. 'Didn't I hear a young lady's voice just now?'

He put his head round the kitchen door and called:

'Come out, duck, we know all about you.'

'Go easy,' Graham said. 'Mrs Grimshaw next door has the sharpest ears in town. And jumps to conclusions.'

'Don't worry,' the milkman said. 'I won't give you away.' He was still teasing. 'Been young myself. A young devil I was, at your age. If you want any lessons, just apply to me.'

'Good-bye,' said Graham.

'Pint every day till Sat'day, eh?'

'That's right. Good-bye.'

– Monday. Five days till they're home. And nights. Five nights, fifty pounds. Monday. Ham rolls and sandwiches for breakfast. A bit dry. But milk washes them down. Stomach seems to be all right now, that's something. Fifty pounds to earn. There'll be some of the money Mother left for house-keeping, too. She won't want any of it back.

– You don't care about money. You know you don't. A matter of people, not money.

– Anyway, I'm committed now. Might as well finish the week.

– Stubborn, boy. That's what you are. Stubborn.

– All right, I'm stubborn.

– Not so busy tonight. No accounting for it. You wouldn't think Monday would be quieter than Sunday. But it is. Eight o'clock and the place empty. All drinking tea, tables cleared, cups washed. Jeff in that cubby-hole of his, doing accounts or something. A chance to talk to Lynn.

'Hi, Lynn.'

'Hi, Prof. How's it going?'

'All right.'

'Put this in the juke-box for me. Let's have "Never come Monday".'

'Monday *has* come. It's here.'

'You're telling me. Never mind, pet. Soon be Tuesday.'

She snapped her fingers, jigged a step or two to the music.

'Want to dance, Prof?'

'Not much room, is there?' he said.

'I've managed in less. Oh hell, here comes Casanova. Sam Bell.'

The big heavy man who'd been in the café on Graham's first night came in. He seemed to be having some difficulty with the door. Then he shambled uncertainly towards the counter.

'Is he drunk?' Graham asked.

'No. Had two or three, maybe. Not drunk. Hi, Sam.'

' 'Lo, sweetheart. What you doin' tonight?'

'Working.'

'You always say that. Come out on the town with me.'

'You always say that.'

'There's plenty more I could say. Here, listen.' He put his lips to Lynn's ear. She giggled.

'Not on your life,' she said. 'Cup of tea, Sam? Cheese sandwich?'

'Aye, that'll do. Look, here's our young friend.' He turned to Graham. 'Delighted to see you again, I'm sure.'

Graham said nothing, but wiped an already-clean table with a cloth.

'Aren't you speaking to me tonight?'

'Good evening,' Graham said.

'Good evening,' said Sam, mimicking his tone. He turned to Lynn. 'I don't think the young gentleman likes me.'

Lynn and Graham were both silent.

'An' you know what?' said Sam. 'I think the young gent should watch out in case *I* take a dislike to *him*.'

Sam Bell had enormous hands. He clenched one of them, the right one.

'Come here, mister,' he said to Graham.

'Take your tea and sandwich, Sam, and sit down,' said Lynn.

Sam looked away from Graham and seemed suddenly to forget all about him.

'You look great tonight, Lynn,' he said.

'Don't I always?'

' 'Course you do. Here, you, mister. Shall I tell you something?' His voice was solemn now. 'She always looks like that. Without fail. Terrific. Don't *you* think she looks terrific, mister?'

Graham reddened.

'Sixty pence,' said Lynn. 'Tea and a cheese sandwich, sixty pence.'

She put out her hand for the money. Sam seized it, pulled her from behind the counter, put an arm round her.

'Lay off, Sam,' she said. She looked annoyed, not frightened. 'That'll do for now.'

'Oh, no, it won't,' said Sam. He put his head close to hers. She drew it away.

Sam's huge hand was spread across her stomach. Anger exploded in Graham. He was half outside himself, watching himself leap forward, swing a fist and hit Sam in the chest. A puny blow, and ineffective.

And on Sam's face, astonishment. And on Lynn's face the same.

Sam withdrew his arm and stared into Graham's eyes.

Graham clicked rapidly back into himself, was terrified, and quailed.

– You're mad. *Mad*. What's it to do with you? Nothing.

– I couldn't stand it.

– Mad. He's lifting his fist. He's going to hit you.

'Jeff!' Lynn shouted at the top of her voice.

Jeff appeared in the doorway from the kitchen.

'What goes on?' he demanded.

Sam's hands dropped to his sides. He still seemed more dazed than anything else. He swayed slightly.

'Out!' said Jeff.

'It wasn't me, it was him,' Sam protested.

'Out!' said Jeff again.

Sam was six inches taller than Jeff and thirty or forty pounds heavier. But Jeff had the tone of command and the boxer's figure. Sam opened his mouth to argue, then closed it again. He turned on his heel and went out, knocking over a chair on the way.

'Did you hit him?' said Jeff to Graham.

Graham nodded.

'Why?'

'The Prof – Graham, I should say – thought he was assaulting me or something,' Lynn said.

'And was he?'

'Not really. Just fooling about. You know Sam. But Graham thought he was.'

'You can go, too,' said Jeff to Graham. 'And you needn't come back. I'm having no fights here.'

'He thought he was protecting me, Jeff,' said Lynn.

'I don't care what he thought. I won't have staff quarrelling with customers. If anyone needs protecting, I'll do it.'

34

'Listen, Jeff,' said Lynn. 'It was sudden. The lad didn't understand. He'll know another time.'

'There's not going to be another time. He's finished here.'

'If he goes, I go.'

'Don't be daft. You know very well you won't.'

'I'll go,' said Graham. His legs were weak. He sat down on the nearest chair.

Two or three customers came in.

'Never mind,' said Jeff. He changed his mind quickly, but his voice was still crisp. 'I'll give you a chance. One chance. But next time you'll be out through that door before your feet touch the ground. Right?'

Graham nodded. Jeff disappeared towards the back.

'Poor old Prof, you're as white as a sheet,' Lynn said. 'Here, have a cup of tea. Alice, what about a drop of something to put in it?'

Alice, still silent, produced a small, flat bottle from her handbag and tipped half its contents into Graham's tea. He drank and began to feel better. Lynn served the new customers and returned.

'You want to watch it, Prof,' she said. 'You won't live long if you go on like that. Sam Bell could eat you for breakfast and still have room for toast. It takes Jeff to deal with fellows like that.'

Graham looked sheepish.

She began to be amused.

'Still, it was as good as the telly,' she said. 'The way you jumped in and biffed him. Only thing missing was a bit of dialogue. You should have said, "Take your filthy hands off her, you swine." '

'I'm sorry it wasn't a good performance,' Graham said. 'I think I'll go after all.'

'No, don't go,' she said. 'I was forgetting how

sensitive you are. Listen, pet, I thought you were great. I did, honest. Nobody ever protected me before. Here, Prof, I mean Graham. Look up.'

Graham looked up. She leaned over the table and kissed him on the cheek. 'There!' she said. 'That's for a good lad.'

More customers had come in.

'Now, Lynn, get on with the job,' said one of them. '*This* job. Cup o'tea and a round o'toast with plenty of dripping on it. And make it snappy.'

Lynn went back to the counter. The café was filling up. Graham got to his feet, still a little shaky, and began collecting crockery again. Soon they were busy.

Time flew. Jeff turned the OPEN notice to CLOSED once more, and they were sitting in the kitchen, drinking tea and smoking.

Lynn was attentive to Graham.

'You all right now, pet?' she said. 'Not sick or shocked or anything?'

Graham shook his head.

'You didn't see what happened, did you, Alice? Old Sam was fooling around a bit, pawing me, you know, the way he does. And up jumps Gray with a sort of "unhand her, villain" look on his face, and wham! Sam doesn't know what's hit him.'

'And in another minute,' said Alice sourly, 'the lad wouldn't have known what hit *him*.'

'It was brave,' said Lynn. 'That's what it was. Brave.'

Lynn stretched across the table, took Graham's hand, and held it between her own two warm ones. She wore pink nail varnish, a bit chipped. Her nails were stubby and not exactly dirty, but not too clean either.

'Nobody ever defended me like that before,' she said. 'Never in my life.'

'I thought you didn't need defending,' said Alice. 'Thought you could look after yourself.'

'That's not the point,' Lynn said. She was still holding Graham's hand. 'You're a pet, aren't you?' she said. 'Nice. And nice-looking, too. He's nice-looking, isn't he, Jeff? Eh? Jeff, I said he's nice-looking, isn't he?'

Jeff didn't deign to reply.

'Bet you have lots of nice little girl-friends,' she said.

'What, me with my spectacles?' said Graham.

'Specs is nothing. Lots of good-looking fellows wears specs.'

She squeezed his hand before letting it drop and picking up her cigarette from her saucer.

'You're a nice little fellow,' she said. 'And not so little. A nice tall fellow, I should have said. And here, I'm interested. *Do* you have a girl-friend?'

Graham hesitated, and blushed once more.

'He does!' Lynn said with delight. 'He does! Look at his face! Go on, Prof, tell us about her. What's her name? What does she look like?'

'Pack it in, Lynn, can't you?' said Jeff.

'No, I can't,' said Lynn. 'Where is she now, Prof? Does she know you're working here? Bring her in to see us.'

'Well,' began Graham. 'Well, she doesn't live around here. Her name's Barbara. She lives on the south coast. I met her when I was on holiday.' He paused.

'Go on!' Lynn said. 'Tell us what she looks like.'

'She's dark,' he said. 'Long dark hair, and a pale skin, sort of creamy. And a very soft voice. And slim.'

'You're making me jealous,' said Lynn.

'I told you, Lynn, pack it in,' Jeff said. 'Anyway, it's time we went.' He stood up.

'I'll see you part-way home,' Lynn said to Graham.

'There's no need,' he said.

'You never know. That Sam Bell might still be hanging around.'

'He won't,' said Jeff. 'He's on the Stoke-to-Cobchester run. He'll be at home in Cobchester by now. As you well know.'

'You can't be sure,' Lynn said. 'Anyway, I'll see the lad part-way home if I want. He looks scared of something. Of course, it could be me he's scared of. Go on, Prof, you're not frightened of *me*, are you? Don't worry, I won't do anything Barbara wouldn't like.'

She was putting her coat on. Out in the street she took his arm.

'Tell me some more,' she said. 'Is she clever?'

He hadn't thought of that.

'Well, quite,' he said. 'Cleverer than me, anyway.'

'*Much* cleverer than me, then. How did you meet her?'

'Oh, just walking on the cliffs.'

'And what did you do together?'

'The usual things. Walking, swimming and all that. Dancing a bit.'

'And she lives down there?'

He nodded.

'You won't see much of her now, then?'

'Well, she has an aunt around here. Her Aunt Susan. She comes to stay here sometimes.'

'How often?'

'Look,' Graham said. 'We've talked a lot about

me and her. What about you? Do you have a boy-friend?'

'Well. Sort of.'

'What's *his* name?'

'Doesn't matter to you, Prof, does it? You're not competing. You're fixed up already.'

'I've told you plenty. You could tell me a bit.'

'Time I was going,' she said.

'Where do you live?'

'No sign of Sam Bell,' she said. 'He'll be home in Cobchester by now, like Jeff said. Mind you, he'll be in again in a day or two, as large as life, but he'll have calmed down by then. Don't get into arguments with him, though. And if he starts getting fresh with me, take no notice. I'll deal with him.'

'I said, where do you live?'

'Oh, I know my way.'

'I expect you do. That wasn't the question.'

'Getting bold, Prof, aren't you?'

'I feel that maybe I ought to be seeing you home, not you seeing me home.'

'I've not far to go.'

'How far?'

'If you must know,' she said, 'I live over the café. It's a living-in job, mine.'

'Oh.' A pause. Then:

'Where does Jeff live?'

'That's his business. Ask him, if you don't mind having your head bitten off.'

'I see,' said Graham.

'Do you?' she said. 'Well, anyway, like I told you, it's time I was going. See you. 'Night.'

' 'Night.'

He'd only walked a few yards when she came running after him. He turned. She held his lapels.

'You were terrific,' she said. 'Thank you again.

But don't try anything more in that line, see? I like you best in one piece. And listen. Whatever happens, don't get into a row with Jeff. *Whatever* happens. Understand?'

'Yes,' he said. 'I suppose so.'

She kissed him, briefly, but on the lips.

'Good-night, Prof, love,' she said. 'God bless.'

Chapter Four

Tuesday. A postcard. View of Bantry Bay. 'Having quite a good time, though it certainly knows how to rain around here. Planning to spend quiet day visiting Glengariff and Garnish Island tomorrow. Hope it's a bit drier. Met a nice English family in the hotel who used to know some friends of Uncle Roger's! Look after yourself, and do eat proper meals. Love, Mum and Dad.' Written by his mother.

– Hell. Should have sent a letter yesterday to that address in Connemara. Better get one off this morning. Hope it's in time. She'll be all worked up if they don't hear from me.

'Dear Mum and Dad, I am getting on very well, though missing you of course. I have done lots of work.'

– Liar, you've hardly done a stroke.

'The weather is about average, quite mild really, but nights are starting to draw in.'

– That's not news.

– Fills a line or two, though.

'I am looking after myself and having good meals, not all fried, and feeling very fit. Have had a few walks and watched some quite nice T.V. programmes. I might go to the cinema with John Wyatt to see a film about a thing from under the earth.'

– Might you?

– Well, there's nothing stopping me. I might.

– And you might not.

'Don't worry, I am doing very well but looking

forward to seeing you on Friday. Lots of love,
x x x, Graham.'

– Nothing about the job.

– Of course not. That's something I'll never tell
them about.

– Because the balloon would go up.

– No. Because I've a right to a bit of my own life.
They don't have to know everything. I don't keep
much to myself. Don't get the chance.

– It's the girl. That's what it's all about. That awful
girl.

– Not so awful.

– She's old. Eighteen at least. Her legs are too
thick.

– She's all right. She stood up for me. She kissed
me, twice.

– And a fine tale you told her. About Barbara.

– Yes. She believed it. She even sounded a bit jealous. Jealous of Barbara, who doesn't exist. A girl of air.

 . . . They were walking on the moors together. A
cool grey windswept kind of day. Her dark hair flew
out like a banner. There was colour in her usually
pale cheeks. It was wild up there, wild and beautiful.
She ran ahead of him. He ran, too, and caught her
hand. They ran together, hand in hand, leaping over
the heather. And then she knew something. He
didn't tell her, she just knew. She got away from
him, ran, ran out of sight . . .

– Barbara, come back, come back.

– Nothing there. This dream is too frail. Gone.

– A girl of air. Gone.

– A girl of flesh. She stood up for me. She kissed
me, twice. Solid. Living.

– Her legs are too thick.

*

'Come right in,' said Alice grimly. 'I can do with you.'

He put on his apron.

'What's the matter? Where's everyone?'

'There's only you and me. And a minute ago there was only me. To do the work of four. So get on with it. You serve.'

'But what's up? Has she – gone?'

' 'Course not. Don't be so dramatic. She's having a night out. Her and Jeff. She made him do it.'

'I don't understand.'

'Plain enough, isn't it?'

'No.'

'Then write me a letter. And meanwhile serve these customers.'

'Aye, get a move on, lad,' said a man waiting at the counter. 'Tea and a pork pie, and I don't want that one in front that looks burnt. And my mate's still waiting for his hot bacon sandwich.'

'All right, don't fuss, I'm doing it now,' said Alice.

It wasn't a busy night, but Graham was fully occupied. He served at the counter and cleared the crockery from the tables. Alice washed dishes as well as cooking. There were many complaints about Lynn's absence. The place didn't have the lively, joke-swapping atmosphere it had when she was around. After closing time at the pubs, the usual bunch of men drifted in. But they munched and swallowed in relative silence, and didn't stay long. When Alice turned the OPEN sign to CLOSED, the café was empty.

She and Graham sat at the kitchen table in the back. Alice was sharp and peevish when Graham put questions to her.

'Does she – do they – often go out like this?' he asked.

43

'What's it matter to you? You'll get paid, same as usual.'

'It's extra work,' he said. 'For you as well as me.'

'I'm used to doing extra,' Alice said. 'Not like her. There's enough fuss if *she* has more to do. And she gets away with it, as often as not. That's the difference between being her age and being mine.'

'But I said, does it often happen? Does she often go out with the boss?'

'That's one way of putting it,' said Alice. A minute went by before she answered his question. Then she said:

'Not often. When she insists. It's a seven-day week here. But you need a break sometimes. Don't I know it? I'm supposed to get my day off, but you wouldn't believe the number of days Jeff owes me.'

Then they arrived. Jeff was wearing a suit. Lynn had on a short coat and a dress. Her scent fought with the greasy smell of the café and won. She'd had her hair done. She looked two or three years older than usual. But she and Jeff both seemed out of temper. Jeff, scowling, disappeared into his cubby-hole, calling to Alice to bring him a cup of tea. Returning to the kitchen table, Alice shoved a second cup in front of Lynn and said:

'Not speaking to each other again, eh?'

Lynn lit a cigarette and didn't answer. Her eyes softened when they fell on Graham.

'Hi, Prof,' she said.

'Hi, Lynn,' said Graham.

'How's my old Prof? I'll miss you when you stop coming here, duck. I will, honest.'

'Thank you,' said Graham.

'I bet you wouldn't treat a girl like some do,' she said. 'You wouldn't go to a club and then spend half

44

the time drinking with your pals and the other half chatting up some other girl. Would you?'

Graham didn't answer.

'Would you?' she insisted.

'N-no,' said Graham.

' 'Course you wouldn't. If you took a girl out, you'd treat her like a lady.' She raised her voice. 'Hear that, Jeff? If the Prof took a girl out, he'd treat her like a lady.'

'Wrap up, Lynn,' said Jeff from the cubby-hole.

Lynn mouthed something in his direction. Then she leaned over the table towards Graham. She might have had a drink or two, but she wasn't tipsy by a long way.

'I envy that girl of yours,' she said. 'What was her name?'

'Barbara.'

'Lucky girl. I hope she appreciates you.' Lynn drew on her cigarette. 'Poor lad, it's a shame she's all those miles away. I bet you could do to get your arm round her.'

Graham reddened and didn't answer.

'He could do to get his arm round a girl,' Lynn called, loudly.

'Well, go on, tell him to get it round *you*,' said Jeff.

'For two pins I would,' said Lynn.

Wednesday night.

She wasn't speaking to anyone. Even Jeff. Even Graham. Even, at first, the customers. She rattled teacups in saucers, slapped sandwiches on plates, took money without a please or a thank you. She scowled at everyone who tried to joke with her.

But this itself became a joke. The place was busy. Lynn was teased on all sides for bad temper and told to cheer up. She had to work harder and harder to

45

keep the sour look on her face and the snappishness in her voice. In the end there were a dozen men around the counter, all trying to make her laugh. She broke down and laughed. The atmosphere grew sociable. Customers stayed, and bought more food and more cups of stewed tea. At closing time the café was still half full and Jeff had to clear the stragglers out.

At the back, in the kitchen over the late-night pot of tea, she fell crossly silent again. Jeff stayed in his cubby-hole. There was no conversation. When Graham got up to go, nobody bothered to answer his 'Good-night.'

But at the doorway Lynn caught him up. She drew a coat round her shoulders.

'I'll walk you home,' she said.

'What's the matter?' Graham asked.

'Oh, nothing. Or everything. Take your pick.'

'Well, it can't be nothing, or you wouldn't have been so fed up all night. Tell me about it.'

'Don't worry, Prof. It hasn't anything to do with you.'

'Why are you walking me home, then?'

'I dunno. I like being with you, Prof. Graham, I mean. You're gentle, that's what it is. Not like *him*.'

'Jeff?'

'Yes, Jeff.'

'What's the trouble with Jeff?'

'Well. What do *you* make of him?'

'I haven't really thought,' Graham said. 'But I reckon Jeff knows what he's doing. A tough character.'

'You can say that again. He knows what he's doing all right. And tough. He's the toughest. Here, Gray, who do you think brings the customers into this joint?'

46

'You do.'

'Right. So why should he treat me like he does?'

'I don't know how he treats you.'

'No, you wouldn't. And I'm not going to tell you, either. You're just a kid. But I'll tell you this. It's nasty, the way he treats me, nasty. And he thinks he only has to lift his little finger and I'll come crawling.'

'Why don't you leave, then?'

'It's not as simple as that. To start with, I live on the premises, see? I'd have to find somewhere to go.'

'It wouldn't be too difficult, would it?'

'No. But that's not all. He wouldn't like it, you see. He'd be nastier still if he thought I was going.'

'You don't have to tell him till you're ready to go.'

'No. But – oh, I don't know, Gray. It's me as well. I left home two years ago. I don't have anyone but him. And he's fine in some ways. Sometimes. When he feels like it. But that's not often, nowadays. He thinks he's got me over a barrel. And maybe he has.'

Graham was silent for a while. They were approaching the corner of his street.

'I still think you should leave,' he said at length.

'I suppose so. I feel things are working up that way. Oh, I dunno, Prof. Sometimes I think it's a hell of a mess, and that's the truth.'

'I'm sorry,' he said.

'I know. I can feel that you are. I wish there was more like you around. Well, I suppose there is, but I'm not likely to meet them. Is this your house?'

'Yes.'

'It's all right, isn't it?'

'I suppose so.'

'What's your old man do?'

'He's an accountant.'

'Not bad, eh? Nearly like being a doctor. And what will *you* do?'

'I expect I'll go in with him. When I've passed my exams. *If* I pass my exams.'

' 'Course you'll pass them. You're clever.'

'Not very.'

'I bet you are. I'm sure you are. Clever, and nice too. Come here.' She kissed him, briefly, as before.

'I've a good mind to kiss you properly,' she said. She giggled. 'That'd shake you.'

'Here, hadn't I better be seeing *you* home now?' he asked.

'Don't be daft. I wanted to come, just for the walk. Time you was in bed, at your age. Off you go now. Hit the trail for dreamland and all that. Thinking beautiful thoughts. Sorry I can't stay and tuck you in . . . Did you say something?'

'No.'

'Oh, well, never mind. Good-night, Prof, love. God bless.'

Thursday. Another postcard from Ireland. View of Killarney. 'Disappointed at getting no answer when we phoned last night, but hope to find letter waiting in Connemara tomorrow. Weather still indifferent. We drove round the Ring of Kerry today but couldn't see much. Had nice lunch, though, for £5.50 each. Hope all is well. Love, Mum and Dad.'

– Damn. You never posted that letter. No use now, they won't get it. And they never said they were going to telephone from Ireland. Or if they did, you weren't listening. How many times will they have rung by now? No telling. There'll be all hell let loose next week.

– It's all because of working at Jeff's. Mad, that's what you were. Good thing it's nearly over. Tonight and tomorrow night, that's all. Then you've finished.

– Trouble or not, I'll miss it in a way.

– You'll miss *her*, you mean.

– All right, I'll miss *her*. And she'll miss me. She said so.

– You'll be well out of it. Think of Jeff. How close is she to Jeff? You don't know, but you have your suspicions. Strong ones. You don't want to tangle with Jeff.

– She's had enough of Jeff.

– Yes. For the moment.

– Not for the moment. For always. Poor Lynn.

– How can she get away from him, anyway?

– I don't know. I wish I could help. Poor Lynn.

'Nasty, the way he treats me, nasty. Thinks he only has to lift his little finger and I'll come crawling. Thinks he's got me over a barrel.'

Poor Lynn, what can I do for you?

'I like being with you, Prof. You're gentle. Not like *him*.'

– I wish I could help.

'You're clever. And nice, too. Good-night, Prof, love. God bless.'

– Poor Lynn, what can I do for you?

Chapter Five

Thursday night.

No Lynn. Jeff at the counter, serving.

Efficient, businesslike. The customers don't like it.

Too efficient, too businesslike. 'One cup of tea. Yes, sir. Coming up. Twenty-five pence. Sausage roll? Yes, sir, fresh today. Forty-five pence. Bacon and one egg, fried? Alice! Bacon and one egg, fried, for the gentleman. Sit down, sir, it'll be ready in a minute.'

No backchat. 'Sir.' They'd rather have 'love' from Lynn.

'Graham, clear up all this mess and get some cups washed. I'm running short.'

Graham put on his apron and started work.

– Quite a busy night. Where is she? Ask quietly, with Jeff around. 'Alice, where is she?'

'Not helping *us*.'

– That's all the answer you get. Come on, Graham boy, get some crockery washed, quick. Splosh in detergent, wash, drain, dry. If you can call it drying, on that horrible damp cloth. Who'd have thought a week ago that you'd learn to wash dishes at this speed? You'll make somebody a good husband some day. Maybe. Ha Ha.

Jeff's voice, floating through from café to kitchen.

'Tea and a ham sandwich. Yes, sir. Tea and a pork pie. Yes, sir. Tea and dripping-toast. Alice! Two rounds dripping-toast. Coffee? Certainly, sir. Won't be a minute. What about that bacon and one egg, fried? Alice! What about that bacon and one egg, fried? Ready soon. Tea and a scone? Sorry, sir, we're out of scones. How about a nice piece of fruit-cake?'

– Still they come. It's hectic. Passes the time, anyway. Half an hour soon gone, an hour. And no Lynn. What's happening tonight?

– She ought to get away from him. No place for a girl. Here with Jeff. Nasty. Lynn, where are you, what goes on?

– Tables loaded with dirty dishes again. Can't get any more on this tray. Don't drop it, for heaven's sake. Floor slippery with spilled tea. No time to wipe it up. Busiest day yet.

Jeff's voice. 'Tea and a piece of pie? Yes, sir. Tea and a Welsh rarebit? Alice! One Welsh rarebit. Won't be a minute, sir. Graham! What about some plates?'

– A lull at last. Two or three customers lingering over their teacups at a corner table. All other tables cleared, all dishes washed. Jeff still at the counter, by himself, reading a magazine.

'He's not talking to us tonight, is he, Alice?'

'He's in a mood, lad.'

'About – Lynn?'

'Sssh. Not so loud. He can hear you through there. Let's have a cup of tea before they come in from the pubs. And what about a drop of something in it?' One side of her face flickered into a wink. She took the small, flat bottle from her handbag and divided its contents between two cups. She and Graham sat down at the kitchen table.

Quietly the door from the living quarters opened.

'Well,' said Alice. 'So you've decided to put in an appearance after all.'

Lynn put her fingers to her lips. She was dressed

51

to go out, not for the café. She wore the short coat around her shoulders and carried a small week-end bag.

She pointed to the other end of the kitchen and raised her eyebrows in a question. From where she was, she couldn't see into Jeff's cubby-hole.

'He's not there, he's in the café,' Alice said, low-voiced.

Lynn tiptoed past them.

'Hi, Lynn,' whispered Graham, but she took no notice. Then she was in the cubby-hole, opening and shutting the drawers of Jeff's desk.

'Here, what you up to?' said Alice. 'Come out of there.'

'Lynn didn't answer. Alice got to her feet and pushed her cup away.

'Are you mad?' she said. 'Leave them drawers alone. Jeff'll kill you.'

'He'll have to catch me first,' Lynn said.

Then Jeff came in from the café. Jeff, alert and lightly balanced as always, walking on the balls of his feet, looking like a boxer in training.

Alice stepped smartly back to the table, sat down, drew her cup towards her. Jeff sat down beside her.

'You can pour me a cup, too,' he said. And then: 'What's the matter?'

Alice didn't say anything. Graham hovered anxiously.

'Alice. I said, what's the matter? Why are you looking like that?'

'He's bound to see you in a minute,' Alice said. She was addressing Lynn, out of sight round the corner. This time she didn't bother to lower her voice.

Jeff turned. Lynn appeared, holding her bag in both hands in front of her. Jeff made no move.

'Come here,' he said quietly.

Lynn stayed where she was.

'Lynn,' Jeff said. His eyes were small and cold. His voice was small and cold. Graham felt a twinge of terror, deep down in his stomach.

'Come here when I tell you.'

'Go to hell,' Lynn said. Her voice sounded shaky.

'Where you going, Lynn?'

'Mind your own business.'

'What was you doing in there, Lynn?'

No answer.

'What you got in your bag, Lynn?'

'My cards. And the wages you owe me. Four weeks.'

'You wasn't thinking of leaving, was you, Lynn?'

'I bloody well was. And am.'

'I wouldn't if I was you, Lynn.' Quietly.

'I'll do as I like.'

'Come here, Lynn.' Quieter still.

She didn't move.

'Come here!' Jeff rapped the words out like a sergeant-major.

In tiny, slow steps Lynn approached him. She looked like a child going to a parent, expecting to be smacked. Then, suddenly, she made a dash for it, was past Jeff and through the communicating door into the café.

Jeff sprang up to go after her.

Graham, white-faced and trembling, not knowing how he got there, was in the way.

'Move,' Jeff said.

Lynn's heels clattered through the café.

'Move,' Jeff said again.

'No,' said Graham.

Behind Lynn the street door crashed.

Graham still barred Jeff's path.

– He'll kill you.

53

– I've got to stay. No choice. Every second helps her.

Jeff raised a fist, lowered it. Then he picked Graham off his feet and tossed him aside. Graham's back hit a table, which slid to the wall behind him and left him sitting on the floor. Jeff was running through the café and out into the street.

'Get out of here, lad, while you've the chance,' said Alice. 'God, you're lucky. If Jeff had hit you . . .'

There was a back door, reached through an outhouse and kept locked. Alice produced a key from a shelf and opened it.

' 'Bye, lad,' she said. 'And this is the end, mind. Don't come in here tomorrow. Go home and stay home.'

Graham heard the key turn as the door closed behind him. He was in a back yard which opened on to an alleyway. In the yard was a dustbin. He sat on it, suffering from shock, his legs weak. For minutes he couldn't have moved if he'd tried.

– No sound from the café. Did she get away?

– Can't guess. She had a start. But not much of one.

– Keep away now, boy. You can't do anything against Jeff. Next time it might be an execution.

– Poor Lynn, what can I do for her?

– Nothing, fool, nothing.

He was still wearing his apron. He took it off, rolled it up, threw it down in a corner of the yard. He wouldn't be needing that again.

His legs were stronger. He walked along the alleyway. It led into a side-street. Graham made his way through this and other side-streets till he came to the road leading uphill towards his home.

He jumped nervously when a figure came out from behind a tree.

'Lynn!' he cried, in surprise and then relief. 'Lynn! You gave him the slip!'

'I did,' she said. She sounded weary. 'I dodged the bastard. Nipped round a couple of corners quickly, and lost him.'

'Will he still be looking for you?'

'How should I know? Might be, might not. But if he is, I reckon he won't come this way. Most likely he'd go down to the station and watch for me there. 'Cause he'd think I wouldn't dare to walk out on him and stay in Crimley.'

'And would you dare?'

'No.'

'What are you going to do, then?'

'I don't know. You tell me, Prof. I need someone like you to think for me. I do everything wrong.'

'I wish you didn't think I was so clever,' Graham said. He shivered. 'And we can't talk about it out here, can we? At this time of night?'

'It's only half past ten,' she said.

'It feels later.'

'Anyway, isn't your house just along this street? And your folks are away, you said?'

'Yes. Only till tomorrow night, though.'

'I'm not thinking about tomorrow night. I'm thinking about the next half hour.'

'All right,' Graham said. 'I'll have to watch out for Mrs Grimshaw next door, though. She'd better not see me bringing a girl into the house.'

'You're not a kid.'

'I am to her and my parents.'

'She's not likely to see us in the dark.'

'She sees *everything*,' said Graham.

But there was no sign of life in the Grimshaw house. He led Lynn up his own driveway and let her in at the kitchen door.

The kitchen contained the boiler and was comfortably warm. Graham seated Lynn at the plastic-topped table.

'What about something to eat?' he said.

'I'm not hungry, Prof . . . Oh, I dunno. On second thoughts, maybe I am. Haven't eaten much today. Funny, you don't feel like it much when you're working in a caff. What you got, love?'

'Beans? Spaghetti? Bacon and egg?'

'Let's have all that,' she said, 'and a great big pot of tea.'

Graham lit the gas.

'Feels just like Jeff's,' he said.

'Oh no it doesn't. This is a home. All the difference in the world. I wanted to see in your home, Gray. Didn't think I would, though. Funny how things work out. Mind if I go and powder my nose?'

'Just along there on your right,' Graham said. He fried bacon and eggs, heated cans of beans and spaghetti.

After ten minutes the meal was ready. He piled the food on big plates and put it in the warming compartment of the stove. Lynn hadn't come back. Another five minutes passed, and then he went in search of her.

She was on an easy chair in the sitting-room. She wasn't settled in it but looked like somebody testing it in a store.

'You got a lovely place here,' she said.

'It's all right, I suppose,' said Graham. 'Just ordinary, like my mum and dad. And me.'

'Seems more than all right to me. Here, can I have a look in the bedrooms?'

'If you like,' Graham said. 'But what about something to eat? It's ready.'

'Won't take a minute,' she said.

In his parents' bedroom at the front, she surveyed the big blue-counterpaned double bed.

'Just fancy,' she said, 'waking up in that every morning. Like a hotel.'

Graham showed her his own room. It had a desk in it, with textbooks spread around. Lynn grimaced. 'Sooner you than me,' she said. She pulled another face at his unmade bed and said, 'Bad lad.' Then they went downstairs to the kitchen.

Lynn ate heartily and finished before Graham.

'Hungrier than I thought,' she said. 'Thanks, Prof.'

'Will you be mother?' he asked.

'What?'

'Pour out the tea.'

'Oh, sure. Here goes.'

Lynn lit a cigarette and sat back. She seemed quite at ease and cheerful.

'Hullo, Prof, love,' she said as if she'd just met him for the first time that day.

'Hullo, Lynn,' he said, 'love.'

'That's better. Hey, Graham, you aren't half looking at me. As if you'd noticed I was a girl.'

'It is quite – noticeable,' Graham said.

She giggled.

'Aren't you sweet!' she said. 'I love the way you put things. Sort of delicately.'

'Listen,' Graham said. 'An hour ago you walked out of Jeff's Café. Hadn't you better decide what you're going to do now?'

'I suppose I should,' she said. She didn't sound worried. 'Got any ideas, Prof?'

Graham shook his head.

'I don't know anything about you,' he said. 'Except that you said you came from Birmingham.'

'As a matter of fact, I was born in Cobchester,'

57

she said. 'Up in the North-West. My family live in Birmingham now. So far as I know, that is. I haven't heard from any of them since I came here.' She drew on her cigarette, reflectively. 'And if you want to know, I don't care if I never see any of them again.'

'Well . . . Maybe you have friends or relations somewhere else?'

'I have friends in London,' she said. 'Sort of.'

'What do you mean, sort of? *What* sort of?'

'Contacts, you might say. People who told me to let them know if ever I hit the big city. Though, mind you, I don't know what they might be thinking of.'

'It doesn't sound very suitable,' Graham said.

'Suitable for what?'

She met his eye.

'I bet your parents talk just like that,' she said.

'They do,' he admitted.

'My life's not like yours,' she said. 'You got to live and let live, Prof.'

'I suppose so,' Graham said. He was silent, looking away from her.

'You've had lots of boy-friends, haven't you, Lynn?'

'Dozens.'

'And –'

'And what?'

'Oh, nothing.'

There was silence for two or three minutes, Lynn stubbed out the cigarette.

'What the hell,' she said resignedly. 'You want me out of here, don't you? All right. I'm just going.'

'But going where?'

'What's it to do with you?'

'I worry about you, Lynn. I care.'

'Nice of you.' She yawned.

'Look, you can stay here tonight, if you like. I'll make up a bed for you. But tomorrow my parents are due home. Can you imagine what they'd say if they came back and found a girl in the house?'

'I'm not too good at imagining, Gray. But I don't stay where I'm not wanted.'

'You *are* wanted, Lynn.'

'Oh, Prof, you look so earnest. Don't *worry* so. I'll be all right. A pity you started asking me questions, that's all. We was getting on fine till then.'

'So far as I'm concerned we're still getting on fine. But you're tired, Lynn. You'll have to stay. We'll talk about things in the morning.'

'Before *they* arrive, hey?'

'Yes. At least I know what time they'll arrive. They can't be early. The crossing from Ireland's at teatime, and they've a three-hour drive at this end. They'll get here about this time tomorrow night.'

'Gray! What was that noise?'

'I didn't hear anything.'

'Sounded like a car. Here, Gray! What if they were a day early?'

'Oh, God. Not that.'

A key turned in the front-door lock.

'It's them!' Graham said. He and Lynn looked at each other and at the window. It had a single opening, narrow and awkwardly placed.

'Can I get out through there?' Lynn asked.

'Not without a struggle,' Graham said.

Mrs Hollis's voice sounded from the hall.

'Graham! Graham! You're not in bed, then?'

'And there isn't time for a struggle!' said Graham. His face was white.

The voice again.

'Graham! We're back! Graham!'

Footsteps approaching. A second to go and nothing to be done.

'Sorry, Prof, love,' said Lynn.

Chapter Six

'I'm afraid my wife gave you a hard time,' Mr Hollis said to Lynn half an hour later, when Mrs Hollis had left the room. 'But you can see how upset she is. The last thing she was expecting on her return home was to find a young lady in the house.'

'She shouldn't have shouted like that, all the same,' Graham said.

'She didn't really mean what she said. She's had a difficult week, Graham. All that non-stop rain, and no letter from you, and nobody at home when she telephoned. And then we had trouble in changing the car-ferry booking, and a long, tiring day today. You must try to understand.'

'What's wrong with *her* trying to understand?'

'Don't speak of your mother in that tone of voice, please.'

'There, there,' said Lynn. ' 'S all my fault. I said I'm sorry. I reckon I got a gift for messing things up. And now, if you don't mind, I'll be going.'

'Going where?'

She said, without hesitation, 'To my dad's house in Birmingham.'

Graham looked at her doubtfully but said nothing.

'It's nearly half past eleven,' Mr Hollis said. 'You won't get a train out of Crimley tonight.'

He thought for a moment, then went on:

'We can't turn you out at this hour. I think we'd better make up a bed for you. I'll see what my wife says about it.'

Mr Hollis went out.

'He'll have a rough passage with that idea,' Graham said.

Lynn rolled her eyes.

'And I'll have some rough passages with both of them later,' Graham added.

'I'd have thought your mum had said enough,' Lynn said.

'Said enough? She's hardly started. She'll be on again tomorrow, and the day after, and next week. I'll never hear the end of this.'

'I told you, Gray, I'm sorry. There's nothing more I can do, is there?'

'Guess not.'

She put out a hand, took his, and dropped it as Graham's mother came in, her lips pressed tightly together.

Mrs Hollis didn't look either at Lynn or Graham. She spoke as if to an invisible third person, somewhere over Lynn's shoulder.

'I'll make you up a bed in the lounge,' she said. 'You can give me a hand if you like.'

'Oh, sure,' Lynn said.

'I'll come and help, too,' said Graham.

'You needn't,' his mother said.

'I will.' His voice was bitter. 'I don't want you telling her off again. She's had enough, and so have I.'

'There's no need to worry. I've said all I have to say to this – person.'

'Oh, for crying out loud,' said Lynn. 'Just let me take my bag and go.'

'No,' said Graham. 'No.'

'He thinks a lot of you, doesn't he?' said Mrs Hollis with chilly sarcasm to the invisible hearer. 'He can't bear to lose your company.'

Mr Hollis came back.

'Now, now,' he said. 'This has been rather distressing for all concerned. But let's be reasonable, shall we? As my wife says, we can provide you with a bed tonight, er – Lynn. And tomorrow morning we'll see you on to the train for Birmingham to rejoin your family.'

'And just for now,' said Mrs Hollis sourly, 'she can be helping me to make up a bed on that settee. If it isn't beneath her dignity.'

Lynn followed her from the room. Mr Hollis closed the door behind them and sat down at the table, opposite Graham.

'And now, young man,' he said. 'Never mind your mother's outbursts, you'll just have to put up with them. But listen to me, carefully. I'm not asking you any questions about what's happened or what might have happened. I shan't mention this episode after tomorrow. I just want to tell you something. You will not, repeat not, get involved with any girl of that type while ever you are in any way dependent on me.'

'What do you mean, of that type?'

'You know perfectly well what I mean.'

'Lynn's all right.'

'From some points of view, possibly so. But from *my* point of view, she is anything *but* all right. How many times have I told you, Graham, that in our profession you should never mix with anyone you'd be ashamed to introduce to your clients?'

'I wouldn't be ashamed of Lynn anywhere. And it isn't *our* profession. It's *your* profession.'

'It will be yours too, Graham, if you'll buckle down to it and pass those exams. As I know you can.'

'As for being dependent on you,' said Graham, 'when will I ever *not* be? I'm dependent on you at

63

school, I'll be dependent on you at college, then I'll be an articled clerk, then I'll be a junior partner if I ever get that far, and you'll be boss all the time. Some prospect!'

'Have I ever been harsh or unfair to you, Graham?'

'Oh no. Not as long as I toe the line. You only want to say who I'll mix with and what I'll do for the rest of my life, that's all.'

'Now, Graham,' his father said. 'Be sensible. I understand more than you think. You're nearly seventeen, you're aware of – of the other sex. I can sympathize with you. I was young myself once, it's quite normal. All I ask you to do is exercise a bit of judgement. Don't pretend you don't know what I mean.'

'I know all too well,' said Graham.

Mrs Hollis came in again.

'Well, that's her ladyship disposed of,' she said. 'I never thought we'd have a guest like *her* in the house.'

She took from her apron a small silver cup and two or three ornaments from the sitting-room mantelpiece.

'Mother!' said Graham, horrified. 'What did you move those for?'

'You can't be too careful,' his mother said. She was putting them in the back of a cupboard.

'You didn't let her *see* you?'

'I made sure she saw me,' Mrs Hollis said with satisfaction. 'She understands now that we know what sort she is.'

'I'll never forgive you for that,' Graham said. 'The things you said, I might. But not that, ever. I hate you.'

Suddenly he was crying.

'I hate you. I hate you.'

*

– God, what a mess. No wonder you can't sleep. You'll never live it down. Your mother won't trust you again. And you won't forgive her.

– She'll be awake. Dad won't. Used to say he could sleep lying across a rope. But *she* will. Eyes wide open, staring into the dark, seeing her boy float away from her. She'll be lying there thinking, thinking. You can feel her thoughts boring into you.

– She wants you all for herself, boy, that's what it is. Her pride and joy, the centre of her world. Her only son. She's jealous. You can't really hate her, can you?

– Yes. For moving the ornaments.

– Imagine her life. Married to your father.

– He's not so bad. At least he's rational. Has a bit of common sense.

– Not so bad in some ways. Worse in others. Rational. Too damned rational. Never mind *her*, think of being junior partner to *him* for twenty years. Hollis and Son, small town accountants. You're the son. Get married, nice little girl like Beth Edwards, have a son of your own. Move up one. After twenty years it's still Hollis and Son. You're Hollis, he's the son. Keep him in order, see he does his work, passes his exams. No getting tangled up with undesirable females.

– Undesirable females. Lynn.

– Undesirable, hell!

– A woman, that's it, she's a woman. Not much older than you, but a woman. Not a Beth Edwards, mincing off to school each day. And not a girl of air, like Barbara. Go back to your Aunt Susan, Barbara. Your imaginary Aunt Susan. You're sacked. Understand? Sacked.

But Lynn. Oh Lynn, what will you *do*?

– Go back to Birmingham, she says. 'The only

place my old man ever pushed me was out. I don't care if I never see any of them again.' Doesn't sound very promising.

– Has friends in London, she says. Friends, sort of. Contacts, you might say. People who told her to let them know if ever she hit the big city. She doesn't know what they have in mind, though. Maybe she can guess.

– All on your own, nowhere to go, wanting a room quick. Oh Lynn, what are you going to *do*?

– She might go back to Jeff. Face it, boy, that's the most likely. They had a row, so what? All over now, finished till next time, kiss and make up.

– Back to Jeff. The boxer's walk, on the balls of his feet. The fear in your stomach when he comes near. Vile, unspeakable Jeff. You hate Jeff, don't you? Really hate him? Not just jealous, loving the same girl?

– Love? Jeff? He doesn't love her. Or anybody or anything. There's no love in Jeff. The small, cold eyes, the small, cold voice.

– And does she love him? 'He's fine in some ways.' What ways? Might mean he's generous when he feels like it. Or might not. Vile, unspeakable Jeff. She can't love him if she walked out on him. But in books they do. Love them and hate them and can't leave them. That's in books. What about life? You don't know about life. How should you know about life?

– Face it, boy. Not the thought about Jeff. The other thought. About you and her. Love was the word. You love Lynn, don't you? You love her. Because she's good. Not good the way your mother would mean, but good. Generous, kind to you. She was sorry she got you into trouble. She'd have walked out into the night if that would have helped.

66

– Still, she certainly did get you into trouble. And how!

– Nonsense, you got yourself into trouble. Be honest, boy, if you can't be anything else. Be honest.

– God, what a mess. Round in a ring, that's how the night thoughts go. Ring a ring of roses, all fall down. You know what you're in for? You're in for life. I sentence you to Hollis and Son for the rest of your days. Pass exams, marry nice little girl, have son of your own, work, retire, die.

– You can't bear it.

– And her? Go to Birmingham, to the father who threw her out? Or London, to all those friends, sort of? Or back to Jeff?

– You can't bear it for her.

– Poor Lynn, what can I do for you?

– Anything. That's what I'd do for you. Anything in the world.

He was dozing off when small sounds made him sit up in bed.

Moving door, feet padding on the carpet, a rustle of clothes.

'Hi,' she whispered.

'For heaven's sake go back to bed. My mother won't be asleep.'

'Poor old Prof.'

'If she hears the slightest sound, she'll be along. And what do you think happens then? All hell let loose. It'll make the row we've already had seem like a tea-party.'

'All right, Gray.' She was still whispering. 'Just came to say good-bye to you, that's all. In case I don't get another chance to say it properly.'

She was kissing him, long and deeply. He thought with horror of his mother, lying wide awake in the darkness, then didn't think at all, then reached out after Lynn as she drew away.

'No. Remember what you said. Good-night, Prof, love. God bless.'

'The young lady,' said Mrs Hollis, 'is still asleep.' She put great stress on the word 'lady'.

'Then I suggest you wake her,' Mr Hollis said. 'If I'm to put her on the Birmingham train, it's time she was moving. Why don't you take her a cup of tea?'

'Take *her* a cup of tea? As if we'd invited her to be here?'

'We did invite her,' said Mr Hollis. 'She offered to go and we suggested she should stay. She's our guest.'

'*You* suggested she should stay,' said Mrs Hollis. '*I* didn't, nor ever would. I don't look on her as *my* guest, I can tell you.'

'But you've made her some breakfast.'

'Just to see her on her way. And the sooner the better.'

'*I'll* take her a cup of tea,' Graham offered.

'Oh no you won't. I'll have her out of there without any cups of tea.'

'Lilian,' said Mr Hollis in a warning tone.

'Don't worry, there's not going to be any unpleasantness. Unless she answers back.'

Graham and his father could hear voices in the next room. Mrs Hollis returned in two minutes, tight-lipped.

'Well, she's coming,' she said. 'But my goodness, the words she used when I woke her, I wouldn't have believed.'

'That's the modern vocabulary, I suppose,' said Mr Hollis.

'It's too modern for me, then,' Mrs Hollis said.

'And for you, too, I should hope, Graham. The things you'd pick up, associating with somebody like that, I hate to think of it.'

Lynn came in, her eyes heavy, without make-up. She was wearing an old dressing-gown of Mr Hollis's.

'Good morning, Lynn,' said Mr Hollis brightly.

' 'Lo,' said Lynn. She yawned, widely. 'Anybody got a fag?'

'I'm afraid we don't smoke in this house.'

'There's some in my bag. Go and get it, Gray.'

'I'll fetch your bag,' said Mrs Hollis, 'if you haven't the energy to fetch it for yourself.'

Lynn stared, pulled a face, then yawned again.

'Would you like some cereal, Lynn?' Mr Hollis asked. 'We have cornflakes, puffed rice, wheat crisps . . .'

Lynn shook her head.

'I'll give you some bacon and egg, then,' Mr Hollis said.

She shook her head again.

'No,' she said. 'Not at this time of day. Just a cup of tea and a smoke, that's all I want.'

Mrs Hollis slapped the handbag down on the table in front of her. Lynn got cigarettes from it and lit up. She sat and smoked in silence, still seeming half asleep. Nobody spoke to her until Mr Hollis said at length:

'I think you should be getting ready if you're going to catch that train. I'll just go and back the car out.'

Lynn was a long time in the bathroom. Mr Hollis tapped a foot, jingled his car keys, and looked at his watch from time to time. He was clearly irritated but didn't say anything. Mrs Hollis stayed eloquently silent. Lynn appeared at last, looking smart again, carrying her week-end bag. She seemed brighter.

'Well,' she said, looking round the three faces, 'here we go.'

'I think you'd better come as well, Graham,' Mr Hollis said, 'and see Lynn on to the train. I have a conference at half past nine and I oughtn't to miss it. And before we go down the drive, just make sure the Grimshaws aren't watching, will you?'

Mr Hollis halted the car in front of the main concourse of Crimley Station.

'You'll just make it,' he said, 'if you get a move on. Goodbye, Lynn. I hope all goes well for you.'

'Thanks for everything,' Lynn said.

'I wondered . . .' Mr Hollis went on. He took his wallet out. 'I wondered whether perhaps a small addition to your financial resources would be in order.'

'I got all I need,' said Lynn.

There was bitterness in her voice.

'You don't have to pay me to go away,' she said.

Chapter Seven

'I reckon I've missed that train,' said Lynn.

'No, you haven't. There's still two minutes to go. You'll catch it if you hurry. The ticket office is just round the corner. Here, let me carry your bag.'

'There's no need, Gray. It's not heavy. Just leave me to it. You don't have to stay.'

'I'll see you on to the train, Lynn. But we'll have to be quick. Come on, we'd better run!'

'I don't feel like running.'

'But, Lynn . . .'

'There'll be plenty more trains, won't there?'

'Well, yes, I suppose so.'

'You in a hurry to see the back of me, eh? Like them?'

'Oh, no, Lynn, no, I'm not. I'll wait with you for the next train.'

'There's no need for that, either. You just run along home and say you saw me off, like they told you to.'

'But I haven't seen you off, Lynn. And you've missed it now. You've definitely missed it.'

Suddenly she relaxed.

'Oh, Prof, love,' she said, 'you look so *worried*. What's bothering you? Do you have to report back to your old man that you actually saw me leave Crimley?'

'No, it's not that, Lynn. It's just that – well, that I care about you. I don't want to leave you hanging about on the station.'

'Seems to me as if *you're* the one that wants caring about, Gray. You're as white as a sheet this morning. Here, now, sit down on this bench. You can stay with me for five minutes if you like. And then I want you to cheer up and go home and forget the whole thing. And get on with exams and stuff. Now, why don't you think about something nice? Like Barbara?'

'Barbara?'

'Don't say you've forgot your own girl-friend.'

'Oh yes, Barbara.'

'When will you be seeing her again?'

'I – oh, I don't know.'

'You don't sound all that eager.'

'I – oh – Listen, Lynn, there never was any Barbara. I invented her.'

'You did what? You mean you made her up?'

'Yes. I don't have any girl-friend. And if you want to know, I never did have.'

'Poor Prof,' she said. 'Poor old Prof. And there was I thinking you were all fixed up, nice and comfortable.'

'All I have is *them*. My father and mother. For ever and ever. Just think of it.'

' 'S not all that hard to find a girl, Gray. Are you scared of them or something?'

'No, I just don't fancy the ones that are around. They're like an extension of my parents, somehow. Same world. It's a slow place, Crimley, slow and stuffy. Takes a long time for new ideas to penetrate. It stifles me.'

'You could be worse off, pet. Much worse.'

'You don't understand, Lynn. My mother holds on to me in one way, my father holds on to me in another. They'll never let go. You don't know what

72

it's like, you couldn't. You're free. The only way I'll escape is to leave home.'

'Don't be in too much of a hurry to do that.'

'I *will* do it one of these days, Lynn. There's times when I can't stand them. Like now. I shouldn't talk this way about them but I can't help it. My mother hiding the ornaments and my father offering you money. I could have sunk through the ground twice over.'

' 'S not your fault, pet. You can't change them, can you? I guess you have to learn to put up with them. Like I do with Jeff.'

'Like *what*?'

'Hey, Prof! Graham! Are you all right?'

'You *are* going back to him, then!'

'Well . . .'

'Don't!' he said. 'Don't go back to Jeff!'

'I'll have to, love. I thought it all over in bed last night. That's why I didn't want to catch the Birmingham train. I didn't mean to tell you. It just slipped out. But what's it matter? Listen, Gray, if I went back home my old man'd only boot me out again. And I know Jeff, I can manage him. It'll all have blown over in a day or two.'

'Couldn't you go somewhere different and make a fresh start?'

'What, all on my own, without anyone? No. That's not me, love. You don't understand. I got to be with somebody.'

'But do you *love* Jeff?'

'I'm used to him.'

'That doesn't sound much good,' Graham said. 'I don't see much future for either of us. Oh, Lynn, I wish it could be you and me!'

'Graham, love! Aren't you nice? But daft. Yes, I

73

wish it could, sort of. Well, I do in a way, maybe. But it can't.'

'Just think. Me getting away from *them*, and you getting away from *him*.'

'Yes. Just think. And think again.'

'But Lynn. *Could* we?'

'Now, now, Prof. Don't start getting these naughty ideas into your head. I'm surprised at you.'

'Lynn, why not?'

'You know why not.'

'Lynn, listen, I mean it, I love you. Let's just get on a train and go. Anywhere.'

'Graham, pet. Oh, Graham, you're lovely but you haven't any sense. What would we use for money, to start with?'

'I have money, Lynn. I've five hundred pounds in my bank account. And about fifty pounds in cash in my drawer, too. I'll go home and get it.'

'And tell your mother you're running off with me?'

'I'll think of something to tell her. Lynn, shall we? Oh, Lynn, let's!'

'Look, they'd catch up with you. And bring you back. And watch over you every minute in future. It's not worth it, love, it's not worth it. If you just want to get your arm round a girl –'

'I don't just want to get my arm round a girl. I want *you*.'

'Maybe so, pet. But don't you see, it couldn't last?'

'There must be some way of making it last,' Graham said. 'Hey, Lynn! What if we were *married*? They couldn't break us up then.'

'What?' she said.

Then she was laughing.

'Graham, love,' she said. 'Graham, sweetheart. Are you proposing to me?'

'Yes.'

'Well, it's a great day. You're the first. Nobody ever proposed to me before. Come here and let me kiss you. No, don't eat me up in the middle of a railway-station. Now, listen to me, pet. Don't make a habit of saying that when you're with a girl, or somebody might take you up on it. For two pins I'd take you up on it myself.'

'Do. That's what I want. I'm serious, Lynn, I mean it.'

'Prof, love, I wouldn't do it to you. Mess up your career and all that.'

'I'm not interested in careers. Accountancy Adding up figures. Anyway, there's work I could do already and be paid for, without going through all that training. I'm ready to work.'

'How old are you, Graham?'

'Seventeen next month. How old are you?'

'Eighteen.'

'Only a year older than me.'

'A year on the calendar, maybe. Years and years older than you, really. I've been around, Graham, you haven't. I ought to look after you. Save you from yourself and all that.'

'Why did you ask, anyway?'

'Well, I can do what I like. I'm grown up by law. You're not. You can't get married at your age unless your parents agree. And maybe it's just as well.'

'I could get married in Scotland,' Graham said. 'Why don't we go to Scotland? Why don't we – run away to Gretna Green?'

Silence.

'Why don't we, Lynn?'

Still silence.

'You've heard of Gretna Green, haven't you, Lynn?'

75

'Yes, Graham. I've heard of Gretna Green.'

'Well, then.'

Silence again.

'What about it, Lynn?'

'Prof, love,' she said. 'Stop tempting me. I'm warning you. Stop.'

'I'm not stopping. Why don't we run away to Gretna Green?'

'Because we can't. Because it's daft. Because it doesn't make sense.'

'It makes sense to me. Beautiful sense.'

'When I was a kid I used to dream of running off to Gretna Green,' she said. 'I thought it sounded terrific. Lovely old village and all the trimmings. Lovely old village blacksmith, under the spreading chestnut-tree and all that. Romantic. And there I'd be, marrying somebody tall, dark and handsome.'

'I'm tall,' Graham said. 'I'm not dark. And I wouldn't say I'm handsome.'

'No, you're not. Still, I wouldn't say you're repulsive, either.'

'Thank you.'

'Not like some I've known.'

'Thank you again.'

'You don't thrill me, though.'

'I'm sorry about that.'

'You're coming on, Prof. You sounded quite sarcastic. I don't like fellows I feel I could walk all over. You don't know much about girls, do you? But I expect you're willing to learn.'

'I'm willing to learn about *you*. I don't care about anyone else. I don't ever want to. I love you, Lynn, that's what I keep trying to say. And I guess I have normal reactions.'

'I noticed that last night.'

'Come here, Lynn!'

'All right, don't grab at me, pet, you don't have to prove it. But don't you think you ought to know a few girls before you start getting fancy ideas like marriage? And listen, Gray, you do understand, don't you? I'm not a good girl, not by any means.'

'Oh, Lynn, you're starting to talk like my dad. I wouldn't have believed it.'

'It's – well, I guess I got to protect you, Prof. Protect you from *me*. Mind you, I got my self-respect, I'm careful, I don't let anything happen that shouldn't. But I wouldn't say I'm good.'

'Lynn, you *are* good, I love you. And listen, Lynn, I can work, and you'd want to work too, wouldn't you? We could have a cottage, just the two of us. Some quiet place in Scotland, maybe.'

'I like somewhere with a bit of life.'

'Well, p'raps we could go to Edinburgh. That's a fine city, and lively too. We could get a little flat, near the centre.'

'I've told you, stop tempting me, Prof. Stop it.'

'I won't. Tempt, tempt, tempt. Come with me, Lynn. Think of it, just us, married. Better than Birmingham, or London, or back in Jeff's stinking café. I'd be good to you, Lynn, I'd do everything for you.'

'Oh, Graham, love, I know you would. You're the nicest fellow I ever met. By miles.'

'I'm not all that nice. But I'd be nice to you. Say yes.'

'I don't know, Prof, I don't know.'

Silence. Thirty seconds, a minute.

She jumped up.

'Oh, to hell with it!' she cried. 'Why not? Let's go! God, what a lark. Off to Gretna, getting married. Graham, love, I'll make you so happy you won't know if you're on your head or your heels.'

★

'You were a long time,' Mrs Hollis said. 'I began to think you must have gone with her.'

'She missed the 9.25.'

'I'm not surprised. It took her long enough to get ready. I thought your father would have died with impatience. He wouldn't stand it from his own family. Anyway, what did she do then?'

'Got the ten o'clock. Change at Stoke. She'll be in Birmingham by midday.'

'I hope all goes well with her.'

'You said that as if you were hoping she'd fall into a vat of boiling oil.'

'I bear her no ill will,' Mrs Hollis said. 'But oh, Graham, how *could* you?'

'Let's not talk about it, Mother. She's gone now.'

'And I must say I'm thankful. Well, what are you going to do now, Graham? Did you get on with any of your maths while we were away? Or were you too busy hanging around that dreadful café?'

'I did some,' Graham said.

'Why not get on with it now? Back to school in just over a week, remember.'

'It's much too fine a day,' said Graham. 'I thought I'd go for a walk, up on the moors. It'll be lovely in this weather.'

'That's all right for *you*, isn't it?' Mrs Hollis said. 'Not like me with the house to clean up after being away a week, and a whole pile of washing, and didn't sleep a wink all night, thanks to your goings-on.'

Graham said nothing.

'I know what's in your mind,' said his mother. 'You want to get away from me until it blows over. Well, let me tell you, Graham Hollis, I may forgive but I'll never forget, ever. Coming back from holiday to a shock like that.'

'I said let's not talk about it, Mother. Can I have some sandwiches?'

'You can make some for yourself. Corned beef in the cupboard, bread in the bin, tomatoes on the bottom shelf of the fridge, will that do?'

'That'll do fine.'

'You've got the right kind of day for it, anyway. Off you go, enjoy yourself, don't think about me. At least it's more like *you* than haunting some horrible café. And healthier, too. You always loved a walk on the moors, didn't you, Graham? I can hardly believe you're the same person.'

'Mother, please!'

'My goodness, you're making plenty of sandwiches. Anyone'd think it was rations for an army.'

'I get hungry in the open air.'

'You haven't lost *your* appetite, have you? I can't eat a thing. I couldn't touch my breakfast.'

'I'll just slip upstairs and put a few things in my rucksack,' Graham said. 'Books, maybe, so that I can rest and do some of my reading in the afternoon. I won't be back until dark. And don't start worrying if I'm a bit late.'

– You're a heel, Graham Hollis. Telling all those lies.

– Got to get a good start.

– They'll be worried to death when you don't come home tonight.

– They'll guess what's happened.

– And then what? It'll break her heart. You'll break your mother's heart. You're a heel, Graham Hollis.

– She can't hold on to me for ever. One way or another she'll lose me sooner or later. Might as well be now. Get it over with. A clean cut.

– But she loves you. You can't treat her like that.

– How does she treat me? How did she treat Lynn? She put the ornaments away. I hated her.

– You don't still hate her?

– No, but . . .

– It's not right, doing this to your parents.

– I'll let them know I'm safe. Somehow, sometime. Have to work it out.

– That won't put things right. Running off at your age without a word of warning!

– They brought it on themselves. Anyway, I'll make it up with them when we're married. When they can't spoil things for us. If they don't come round it's their own fault. When we're married . . .

– You don't have to marry her, boy.

– But that's what I want. Married, safe, they can't touch us then. *Fait accompli.* Married. I love you, Lynn. No more Jeff, nothing like that, ever. Just us, married.

– Get a move on, then. She'll be tired of waiting. What if she's gone?

– She won't. She might. She won't. Wait for me, Lynn. I'd wait for ever for you. Where's that bank book? Five hundred and ten pounds. Plenty of people marry on less. Hurry, boy, hurry. Get a few things together quickly. God, how that rucksack bulges. Mother'll wonder. No, she won't. Anorak, walking-shoes, she's seen me go off like this a score of times. Don't look guilty, that's all. Right? Right. Here I come, Lynn. Wait for me, wait for me. Won't know if I'm on my head or my heels. Don't know it now, for that matter. Make me happy, Lynn. I'll do anything for you. Coming, Lynn, love, coming.

Chapter Eight

She was waiting in the station entrance.

'I thought –' he said.

'I thought –' she said in the same moment.

He grinned. She giggled.

'I thought you'd changed your mind,' he said.

'That's what I thought about you. Or else I thought your mum had grabbed you and locked you in the cellar.'

'You haven't changed your mind, have you, Lynn?'

' 'Course I have. Changed it half a dozen times. And I might change it again in a minute. So watch out.'

'You wouldn't, Lynn. You wouldn't. Would you?'

'Oh, Graham love, you look so *funny* when you're worrying. Stop it now. I made my decision. We're in business. But listen, pet, if *you've* thought better of it, now's your chance to bugger off home and no more said. I'm not leading you astray, Prof. You're leading me astray.' She giggled again.

'I'm not leading you astray,' he said. 'We're going to get married, Lynn. M-A-R-R-I-E-D, married. And live happily ever after.'

He put his arms round her. She breathed warm breath into his ear.

'That tickles,' he said.

She did it again.

'It tickles like mad.'

She was pressing herself against him.

'I guess your reactions *are* normal,' she said. 'Hey, Prof, I was going to tell you something. Listen carefully.'

She whispered, with more warm breath in his ear:

'I love you, Graham. I do, honest. I love you more than I ever loved anyone. Except a little dog I once had, called Butch, that died.'

'Thank you!'

'Of course, he was only a dog, you're a person, that's different. But you know what I mean. He didn't want anything off me, he wasn't on the make, he just loved me, and I loved him.'

'And *we* love *us*.' He was kissing her.

'Come on, Prof,' she said. 'If we're going places, it's time we was starting.'

'It is, too!' he said. 'You take my mind off things. Sooner we get away from here the better.'

'Bonnie Scotland, here we come!' said Lynn. 'How'll we get there, Gray? I was looking at the timetable while you were away, but there don't seem to be no trains going up there from here. Will we have to change?'

'I think it'd be a good idea if we didn't go by train at all,' said Graham. 'Let's go by road instead.'

'Oh, sure,' she said. 'Let's see, love, where did you park the Jaguar?'

'I'm serious. We can hitch.'

'If you're worrying about the price of tickets,' she said, 'don't! I got a bit of money too, Gray. I don't mind spending it.'

'I wasn't thinking about what it'd cost,' Graham said. 'I was thinking that in a few hours' time people are going to come here asking questions. And I dare say we've been noticed. A couple hanging around the station for quite a while, the way we've been.

And if we buy tickets here they might remember us at the booking-office.'

'Aren't you clever, thinking of that?'

'So why don't we throw them off the trail?' Graham said. 'Look, let's make sure we've been seen. We'll go to the bookstall and the refreshment room. And then let's go to the inquiry office and ask about trains to London. And talk and laugh a lot and ask plenty of questions. And then we'll sneak quietly away. You can go to the Ladies and out by the side entrance into Mill Street, and I'll go the other way through the car-park into Town Square.'

'When did you work all that out, Gray?'

'On the way to our house and back, just now. Then we'll get the bus – separate buses – along Liverpool Road as far as Scannell. And then we can join up and start hitching. Twenty miles west to the motorway intersection, then off we go, due north for the Border. We'll be in Scotland tonight!'

'Gray, you're a flipping genius. You're getting me all excited. Come on, let's go. The road to Gretna Green!'

'And beyond. The road to Edinburgh, too. It's lovely there, Lynn. You'll like the shops. And the castle, sort of brooding over everything, all grim and frowning. Romantic. Makes me feel like Young Lochinvar.'

'Young who?'

'Lochinvar. Somebody in a poem that ran off with a beautiful girl. And married her. Just like us.'

'Oh.'

'Flung her across his splendid steed and galloped off.'

'We wouldn't get far, two of us on a blooming horse, would we?' Lynn said. She giggled again. 'Still, you got it all worked out, Prof. I'm glad I'm with you. Hey, it's a lovely day out there. I reckon we're going to have fun. I feel good, don't you? I feel terrific. Just think, bashing off to Gretna like Young Thingummy. Graham, pet, you do get some lovely ideas. What it is to have brains . . . Now, now, that'll do. We can't stand here dilly-dallying.'

'Oh yes we can,' Graham said. 'That's part of the plan. See that porter coming? What you have to do now is give me a nice kiss, just timed right, so that he'll see it and remember us. And then we'll go and kiss in the refreshment-room, and then at the book-stall, and then at the inquiry office . . .'

'You're coming on fast, aren't you, Prof?' she said.

She got off the bus at Scannell, on the Liverpool road.

'Thank heaven you're here,' Graham said. 'I thought I'd lost you or you'd changed your mind after all. I was expecting you to be on the next bus after mine. Can you imagine how I felt when you weren't on that, or the one after it either?'

'Now, Prof, keep calm. Your voice is shaking.'

'Sorry, Lynn, I couldn't help it. I care so much, that's what it is. If you didn't come now, I think I'd kill myself.'

'Don't be so daft, love. You wouldn't. Anyway, don't *worry* so. I don't let fellows down, honest.'

'Never mind about other fellows, don't let *me* down, that's all. Oh Lynn, I'm so thankful you've arrived, you wouldn't believe it. What happened?'

'I saw a jumper I fancied in a window, while I was waiting in Town Square. Five pounds fifty in a sale. So I bought it. It'll suit me a treat. Can't wait to try it on.'

'I like you whatever you're wearing.'

'That's not the thing to say, Prof. You should say,

"*I* can't wait to see it on, either. I bet it looks terrific on you." That's what you ought to say.'

'All right, I bet it looks terrific on you. But we'd better be on our way, hadn't we? Let's just get beyond Scannell village, then we'll try and hitch a ride.'

'Wait just a minute, love.'

She drew the jumper from her bag and held it up against herself.

'There, what did I tell you?'

'Yes, it does suit you,' Graham said. 'Here, let me buy it for you. A present.'

'No need, love. I told you, I got some money, you don't have to spend yours.'

'I *want* to buy it for you. I haven't given you anything yet. I want to give you something.'

'There, aren't you sweet? But I wasn't expecting you to buy it for me. Honest I wasn't, Gray. I don't go with fellows for what I can get out of them. I'll buy *you* a present, though, soon as I get a chance. What would you like?'

'I don't want anything,' Graham said. 'I've got everything I want in the world already. You.'

'You're happy, pet, are you?'

' 'Course I'm happy,' Graham said. 'Oh, Lynn, I love you, love you, love you.'

'I believe you. I'd believe you even if you only said it once.'

'Still, I think we should be moving on.'

'All right, Prof, we're on our way. Quick march.'

'Let's start hitching now,' Graham said.

'What time is it, love?'

'Half past twelve.'

'Feels later. I'm hungry.'

'I'm not surprised, seeing you only had a cup of tea for breakfast.'

'That's all I ever have. But I'm hungry now.'

'Good, we'll have a picnic. Just over this wall, eh? Nice and warm in the sun. And *then* we'll look for a ride.'

'Okay, Prof. What you got in that rucksack of yours?'

Graham brought out food and a flask of coffee. They ate sandwiches and tomatoes together, biting alternately. He peeled a banana and they nibbled it from each end until their lips met in the middle. They drank coffee. Lynn lay back, hands clasped under head.

'I told you we'd have fun,' she said. 'This is great. I wonder how Jeff's getting on.'

'Don't think about Jeff,' he said.

She sat up.

'I'm going to try that jumper on.'

'What, now?'

'Why not? Close your eyes.'

He closed his eyes.

'You're peeping.'

'I'm not.'

'I bet you are.'

'I'm not, truly.'

'Well, why aren't you, then? You *are* slow.'

He opened his eyes. She was pulling the jumper into position.

'There. Do you like it?'

'Yes. It does suit you. It . . . sort of clings, doesn't it?'

'They're meant to, this kind. Of course, you need to have something for them to cling to . . . Oh, Prof, I love the way you blush.'

'I wish I didn't.'

86

'You'll get over it. I think I'm going to keep this on. Should be useful for hitching.'

They climbed the low stone wall and were back at the roadside.

'This could take a while,' Lynn said.

But they had only waited two or three minutes when a small grey van with a ladder fastened to the top of it drew up.

'Hi, Lynn,' a voice said. 'Goin' my way?'

'Oh Lord. That's Charlie Booth. Fancy him coming along just now.'

'Who's he?'

'A customer. Comes into the café sometimes.'

'What do we do, Lynn?'

'We climb in,' she said. 'What else can we do?'

They got into the van and sat side by side in the front, squashed up together. Behind them were cans of paint, brushes and buckets.

'Where you want to be, Lynn?' Charlie asked.

'We're heading for the motorway.'

'You're in luck. I'll drop you at the intersection.'

Charlie whistled an old pop-tune as the van picked up speed. He was a small, thin, round-faced man in early middle age, wearing overalls.

'Fine day for a ride,' he said at length.

'Mmmm.'

'Your day off, Lynn, is it?'

'Well . . .'

'I seen your pal before. He was helping in the caff the other night. That's right, isn't it, lad?'

'Yes.'

'You wouldn't remember me, with so many being in the place. But I remember you. Got a good memory for faces.'

'Well, now you can start forgetting, Charlie,' said Lynn. 'Forget you've seen us. Okay?'

The van swerved slightly.

'Hey, Lynn, what you up to?'

'Never you mind.'

For a minute or two Charlie whistled his tune and said nothing. Then:

'If you want me to forget I've seen you, I reckon you should tell me why.'

'Just a case of minding your own business,' Lynn said.

'I don't get it, Lynn. I don't get it.'

'You're not supposed to get it.'

'Then why am I supposed to keep quiet?'

Lynn groaned.

'Listen, Charlie,' she said. 'I left the job. Jeff won't like it. And I don't want him to know which way I've gone. Will that do for you?'

'I reckon so,' said Charlie. 'And what about the lad?'

'What about him?'

'He's the new boy-friend, eh? Picking 'em young these days, aren't you, Lynn?'

'He's over eighteen, that's what matters.'

'He doesn't look it to me.'

'Charlie, will you do as I ask and forget you've seen us?'

'Oh, I reckon so,' Charlie said. 'I don't owe Jeff Wright anything. I won't tell him. Which way you going, Lynn, when you get to the motorway?'

'What's it *matter*, Charlie?'

'Doesn't matter at all. I was just interested. Don't tell me if you don't want.'

'We're going south as a matter of fact. Going to London.'

'Have a good time, then. I been to London once. Went to the Zoo. Didn't think much of it. Not as good as Chester. Hey, Lynn, did you ever hear the one about the Englishman, the Irishman and the Scotchman what went up to London for the Cup Final?'

'No, Charlie. Tell us it.'

'Well, it's a bit of a long story.'

'That's all right, go ahead.'

'Well, there was these three fellows, see, and they was looking for somewhere to have a meal . . .'

'At least it stops him asking questions,' Lynn whispered into Graham's ear.

'Do you trust him?' Graham whispered back. 'Will he really not tell Jeff?'

'Oh, I reckon Charlie's all right. What's it matter, anyway? The main thing is to put plenty of miles between us and Crimley.'

'It'd be a pity if all that performance on Crimley station was wasted.'

'Get away with you, Gray. You enjoyed it.'

'Lynn! You're not listening!' Charlie complained.

'We *are* listening, Charlie, love,' said Lynn. 'Go on.'

'So the Scotchman says, "Hoots, mon, awa' wi' ye, ah'm not spending ma money, I brought ma own!" '

'Ha, ha, ha,' said Lynn.

'That's not the end,' said Charlie. 'That's only the middle.'

'All right, Charlie. Go on. Tell us it to the end.'

Chapter Nine

'Hot, isn't it?' Graham said. 'For September, I mean.'

' 'S a lovely day, pet. We couldn't have picked better.'

'I wish somebody'd stop.'

'I told you, Gray, you have to be patient at this game. Specially at a place like this. Lots of drivers don't like stopping just before they go on to the motorway. But there's no hitching *on* it, so we got no choice. Somebody'll pick us up sooner or later, somebody always does . . . Hey, Prof, are you all right?'

'I'm fine.'

'You look a bit bothered. Are you *sure* you're all right?'

'Well . . . to tell you the truth, Lynn, I've got just a bit of a headache. I never thought of bringing aspirins. You wouldn't have any, I suppose?'

'Sorry, love, I don't carry 'em. Never get headaches nor nothing. Strong as that flipping horse of Young Thingummy's, I reckon . . . Poor old Prof, is it bad?'

'It's nothing, really.'

'Look, why don't you sit behind that sign, where there's a bit of shade? And let me do the hitching. I might get quicker results.'

'That doesn't seem fair to you, Lynn.'

' 'Course it's fair. You just settle down. I'll sing out when we get a ride.'

– It's not really happening.

– It *is* happening, it damn well is.

– Here behind a great big sign, all about motorway restrictions. On a grass verge, in heat, with flies around. It's not happening, it can't be happening.

– It is, is, is, is, is, is.

– Oh, my head.

– There's time to go back.

– Don't be daft.

– Of course there's time. Get a lift easily. Back to Crimley, never missed.

– And leave her? Back out on her now? When it was all your own idea?

– She'd understand. 'Okay, Prof,' she'd say, 'if that's how you feel, run along home, don't mind me.' She wouldn't fuss.

– Well, what are you waiting for? Pack it in while you have the chance.

– Drop Lynn? Oh no. It's *because* she'd understand, that's why I won't drop her. Ever.

– You're not the first, you know. Or the second.

– I don't care.

– Or the last.

– I might be. I will be. We'll be married, that's different. She said she loved me, she never loved anyone else, this won't be like anything else for her either. She's good, we'll love each other always.

– Her legs are too thick.

– I don't love her for her legs. She's good . . . Somebody's stopping. About time, too. He's leaning from the cab, they're chatting. Looks as if we might be fixed up . . .

'C'mon, Gray, we got a ride at last. But you'll have to go in the back, pet. The driver's not too thrilled at having you at all. He thought at first there was only me. 'S no use me offering to swap places with you. He wouldn't fancy *that*.'

'I don't mind where I go, Lynn. So long as we're on our way.'

— Easier said than done, though, getting in the back of a truck like this with the tailboard up. Even if you're tall, like me. One leg over, that's something. Oh, the clot, he's moving off. It'd all be the same to him if I just fell into the road. He wouldn't know or care. Hold on tight, hold on, hold *on*, boy. Phew, only just made it. Plenty of room inside, anyway. Dark, though. Have a look through the back. Motorway starting to peel away behind us. A slow thing, this, but can't be choosy. Heading north at last. The road to Scotland.

— You've done it now, boy. No turning back. You'll never make that driver hear, even if you try.

— All right, I've done it. So what? It's what I wanted to do. She's done it, too. She's still with me.

— You're scared.

— Yes, I'm scared. Oh, my head. But going through with it. I love her, love her, love her. We're on the road to Scotland. Wonder how far this truck's going. Stuffy in here, and warm. You wouldn't think it could be so warm.

— In another hour or two you'll be missed.

— Another hour or two. That's a long time. It's been a long day. And a long night before it. And a long week before that. My head. Going round and round. She loves me, she said so. Never loved anyone else. Only a little dog called Butch. Come here, Butch, good dog, sit. Lie. Warm in here. Dark. A long, tiring week. On the road now. I could fall asleep, easily. I won't, though. I won't sleep. Definitely I won't sleep. No sleep. Not at all. No sleep. No sleep. No.

★

'Wakey, wakey. Rise and shine.'

'Ugh?'

Graham raised himself on an elbow.

'Wake up, love, we've arrived.'

A yawn.

'What time is it, Lynn?'

'Nearly eight.'

'At night?'

'Sure it's at night. You been fast asleep, love. It was a shame to wake you. You looked sweet. But we got to get out now.'

'Where are we, Lynn?'

'Well . . . we're not quite where you was expecting. We're at Pool-on-Sea.'

'We're *what*?'

'At Pool-on-Sea.'

'That's not on the way to Scotland.'

'It is, sort of, pet, isn't it? Well, it's nearer to Scotland than what Crimley is. At least I think so.'

'I suppose it is,' said Graham. 'A bit nearer. But why Pool-on-Sea?'

' 'Cause that's where Bill's depot is.'

'Bill?'

'Bill what gave us the lift. Hey, Bill, come and meet Graham.'

'How do, Colonel?' said Bill. He was a tall man, as tall as Graham and nearly as thin. 'Sorry I hadn't room for you in the cab. But I been hearing all about you. Some folks have all the luck. You got quite a girl there, mate.'

Graham climbed down from the truck.

'You two knew each other, then?' he said.

'No,' said Lynn.

'Yes,' said Bill.

'Well, he *says* he's talked to me in the café,' said Lynn. 'But I don't believe him. Tell anybody anything, he would. Wouldn't you, Bill? I know your type.'

'You know all types, don't you?' said Bill.

'Most of 'em. I know more than you think. I know you're married, for instance.'

'How do you know?'

'Never mind, I just know. *And* you got kids.'

'That's right. Three. You must have second sight.'

'I have. You develop it, working in a place like Jeff's. Well, now, just you go straight home to them kids, see? And thanks for the ride, Bill.'

Bill pulled a face.

'Cheerio, Colonel,' he said. 'Keep her in order.'

He drove off.

'There, Graham, pet,' said Lynn. 'How are you? How's your head?'

'A bit better, I think,' said Graham. 'But, Lynn, *why* did you take a lift to Pool-on-Sea?'

'I thought it was time we got away from that blasted intersection. We might have waited long enough for a ride to where we was really going. And I haven't been to Pool-on-Sea for at least two years. And there's lots of places to stay, with no questions asked. And nobody'd ever find us here. We could do a lot worse than Pool-on-Sea, Gray.'

'My auntie and uncle live at Pool-on-Sea,' Graham said. 'I might have been on holiday here all this week.'

'Lucky thing. Why weren't you?'

'I didn't want to come. And I'm glad I didn't. I'd never have met *you*, Lynn.'

'Might have been all the better for you, pet. You wouldn't have been on a daft lark like this, would you?'

'I don't call it a daft lark,' said Graham. 'I'm seri-

94

ous. You're serious, Lynn, aren't you? You will marry me?'

' 'Course I'll marry you. Over and over if you like. Oh, cheer up, Prof. I don't like you with that long face. It reminds me of your old man. Come on, pet, enjoy yourself, that's what I'm going to do. You know what that is, over there? Where all them lights are?'

'It's the pleasure beach,' said Graham.

'That's right. Jeff was always going to bring me, but he never got round to it. Likes making money better than he likes spending it, that's Jeff. Oh well, here we are. What we waiting for, Prof? Let's go.'

'Hungry, pet?'

'I – no, Lynn, I don't think I am. Not yet. Not very.'

'I am. I could eat that flipping horse we was talking about. *That'd* let you down, if you was Young What-sit and your girl-friend ate the flipping horse. Here's a hot-dog stall. Two hot-dogs, two cokes, please, mate. I'll eat some of yours, Gray, if you can't man-age it. *What* did you say his name was?'

'Who? Oh. Young Lochinvar.'

'And his girl-friend? What was *her* name?'

'I'm not sure. Oh, yes, I remember, Ellen.'

' 'S a bit like Lynn, isn't it?'

'I suppose it is. Graham's not much like Lochinvar, though.'

'No. Never mind, pet. You got the same idea.'

'You know what, Lynn? You never told me what your full name is.'

'Linda, that's what they gave me to start with. I changed it to Lynn. I like Lynn better, don't you? More modern.'

'And your other name?'

'Smith.'

'What?'

'I said Smith. Here, love, are you going to eat that hot-dog or aren't you?'

'I don't fancy it, somehow.'

'Give it here. Let me finish it. You're not drinking your coke either, are you? Better just leave that, pet. I'm not having two bottles of coke or I'll be in and out the Ladies all night. *Sure* you're all right, Gray?'

'Yes. Positive. I feel fine now.'

'What shall we go on first? Himalaya Ride? Sky-wheel?'

'I don't mind at all, Lynn.'

'Oh, look, funny hats! How'd you like me in a funny hat, Gray? You wouldn't, would you? Don't worry, pet, they're things you wear when you're in a crowd. I worn them in my time, but not now. Which do you like best, the one that says "Boy Wanted" or "Kiss me Slowly"? All right, not "Boy Wanted", I got one already, haven't I, love? And you can kiss me slowly any time, can't you? Not now, though. Oh, and listen to that! The Laughing Man! I remember him from when I was here before.'

On a pedestal in the middle of the crowd was a figure of a fat man, over life-size, rolling from the hips, laughing, laughing.

Ha ha ha ha ha ha ha

Ha ha ha ha

Ha ha ha

Haha haha haha haha ha ha ha

A-ah-ah-ah ha ha ha

O-oh-oh-oh ho ho ho

Ha ha ha ha ha ha ha . . .

People came up, stared, grinned, laughed in turn. Scores of people, laughing. Lynn laughed and laughed, clung to Graham helplessly, laughing.

Graham's face creased reluctantly. He was grinning. He was laughing. Not amused really but laughing, laughing.

'That's better, love. Does you good, doesn't it?'

They were both laughing, both helpless now. People all round, laughing. The fat man looming over all, laughing.

Ha ha ha ha ha ha ha

Ha ha ha ha

Ha ha ha

Haha haha haha haha ha ha ha

Ah-ah ah-ah ha ha ha

O-oh-oh-oh ho ho ho

Ha ha ha ha ha ha ha . . .

Tears rolled down Lynn's cheeks.

'C'mon, love,' she said at last. 'Got to get away, it's killing me.'

– Dark now. Lights, coloured lights, millions of lights. Music everywhere, blaring in competition. People, people, people, people.

– And rides. Don't feel much like going on rides tonight. Head still aching, stomach queasy. But better not chicken out. So here goes.

– Log run. Hollow plastic log, sit in it, carried on great, swooping, swirling watercourse, throwing up spray, up, down, round, splash, up, down, round, splash, up, down, rou-ou-ound, finished.

– Himalaya ride. Up, up, up, up, round, round, slowly, slowly, see all the lights, moon coming up, shining on sea, pier, esplanade, round, round, slowly – plunge! Phew, stomach dropped out, ugh, up, up, round, plunge! All cling, shriek. Up round plunge up plunge up plunge plunge plunge. Up, round, do-ow-ow-own, rou-ou-ou-ound, finished.

– Octopus. Writhing limbs of coloured lights, looks as if it could get away, chase people, eat them.

Locked into cell at end of limb, go round and round, head over heels over head over heels over head over u-u-u-u-ugh, this is hell, they love it, it's hell, can't stand it, head over heels over head over heels over head over finished.

– Skywheel. Must we, yes we must, got to keep up, she's enjoying it, she hasn't noticed . . .

'You *sure* you're all right, love?'

'Yes, Lynn, of course. This is fun, isn't it?'

'You look white, Graham. White as a sheet. How's your head?'

'Not so bad.'

'You better have a rest. I ought to have seen you wasn't well.'

'I *am* well.'

'Let's get some fish and chips and eat them sitting down, nice and quiet.'

'I'm still not hungry, Lynn.'

'You're not feeling sick, too, are you, Gray?'

'No, not at all. Not the least bit.'

'You might be better if you ate something. It's hours since we had that picnic. Sit there and take it easy . . . Look, I brought fish and chips and some orange drink as well. Makes you thirsty, a place like this. Is it nice, pet?'

'Yes, thank you.'

'Well, you've ate most of it after all. Feeling better now?'

'Much better.'

'Let's not go on no more of them big up-and-downy things. I'm not sure that I like them myself. Not too many in a row, anyway. We'll stick to the gentle ones, eh?'

– Ghost train. A quiet ride, comparatively. Skel-

98

etons looming up, clammy things dangling over your face. Weird moanings and groanings, good for a giggle. Stomach not too good, though.

– Amusement arcade. Rows of machines. Roll coins down chutes, try to push pile of them off edge of platform. Pin-tables, score a million and get your money back. Try to pick up prizes with mechanical grab, miss every time. Oh no, Lynn, not a hamburger, no, not for me, Lynn, no, no, no.

– Mirror maze. Walk into it, lose each other at once. Walls of plate-glass, walls of looking-glass, walls you can walk through, walls you can't. Lynn, Lynn, it's a long time since I saw you. Lynn, Lynn, are you still in here? Run, boy, run. Don't be silly, of course she's here. Where? Can't see her. Oh, there you are, Lynn, I wondered what had happened to you, yes, I know I'm daft, Lynn, I can't help it, yes, I know.

– Football game. Gang of lads kicking real footballs at knockdown figures of well-known players, trying for a prize. Sit down, Graham boy, your stomach's heaving, this is bad, are you going to throw up? No. The lads want Lynn to have a go. She won't, though. Yes, she will, of course she will. Hasn't any idea of how to kick a ball. Missed. Missed again. Oh! Over goes the smallest figure, a bespectacled referee. Cheers from all. A prize for Lynn, toy animal of some kind. Chatting her up, now, the lot of them. Six boys and a girl. Oh, she's enjoying herself, her head's all right, her stomach's all right, she's as strong as that flipping horse. Young Lochinvar, ha ha. She's in her element. *She's* all right, Jack.

– My head. My stomach.

'Graham, sweetheart! You're ill. You ought to be in bed.'

99

'I'm not so bad. Better than I was a few minutes ago. Go on, Lynn, enjoy yourself, I'll be all right.'

'No, pet. I'm sorry. I knew you wasn't well, I should have stayed with you. All right, fellows, thanks, that was fun. 'Bye, all. There, now, Gray. Look, I won a little dog. Nice, isn't he? I'm going to call him Butch, after the little dog I used to have. He's not the same sort of dog, though. Butch was a Heinz. Fifty-seven varieties and a few over. Just rest for a few minutes, Graham, there's no hurry, we're not going nowhere.'

'I tell you I'm feeling better, Lynn. And what do you mean, we're not going anywhere?'

'Well, we're not going anywhere *tonight*, pet, I can tell you that. Not in the state you're in.'

'What are we going to do, then? It's half past ten.'

'We'll find a place to stay. It's past the main holiday season. There'll be lots of empty rooms around. I better get my wedding-ring out of my handbag.'

'Your *wedding-ring*?'

'Yes. You never heard of a wedding-ring before?'

'But how do you come to have one? Lynn, you're not married, are you?'

'Don't look so startled, love. 'Course I'm not married. I'd have told you if I was.'

'Then how do you come to have a wedding-ring?'

'I have a wedding-ring because I bought one. Fifty pence at a market stall, if you must know.'

'But why –?'

'Because there's times in a girl's life when it comes in handy to have a wedding-ring, see? Like now.'

'But, Lynn –'

'Because you want looking after, pet. Because you look like death warmed up. I got to put you to bed. Look, we'll find some little place with a fancy name, there's plenty just round the corner, and the sooner we get you off your feet the better. I told you, my name's Smith, so you can be *Mr* Smith, right? What you need is somewhere nice and warm with a bathroom close by.'

'Yes, Lynn.'

'And you need it pretty quick, don't you?'

'Well – yes, Lynn.'

'Right. Well, here we are. Rochester Hotel. Sounds better than it looks, but I dare say it'll do.'

– You're going to throw up.

– No.

– Yes.

No. Swallow hard. No.

– Yes.

– No. No. Not in front of her. Wait till she's out of the room.

– Yes. Get to that basin, quick.

– No. Oh God, no. No, no, no. Yes.

'Sorry, Lynn. Oh, I'm sorry.'

'Never mind, pet. I knew it was coming. I'm glad we got here in time. It was a bad do, wasn't it? You're shaking.'

'I'm all right now.'

'Do you often come over like this, Gray?'

'Sometimes. If I'm upset or excited. But not all that often. Honestly, Lynn, not all that often.'

'Poor old Prof. Don't worry, it doesn't bother me. I'm only sorry for *you*, you look so miserable. Anyway, I'm glad you got it over with. Here, let's get you into bed, nice and warm, that's what you need. Don't be shy . . . You *are* thin, aren't you?'

'I guess so, Lynn. I can't help it.'

'Still, it's better for a man to be thin than fat.'

'Lynn.'

'What is it, Gray?'

'When we get married, I want you to have a proper wedding-ring. Made of solid gold. To last for ever.'

'That'd be lovely.'

'Because I want us to be married to each other for the rest of our lives. Don't you?'

'Well, it's a nice idea, pet.'

'I'll love you always, Lynn.'

'But Graham, I'm not good enough for you.'

'You are good, Lynn. You're good all through. Like that ring.'

'Which one, pet?'

'That solid gold one.'

'You do say the loveliest things, Gray. Know what? I love you, too. More even than Butch.'

'That's nice, Lynn.'

'Happy now?'

'Ever so happy. Are you?'

'Yes, pet. I thought we was a bit daft to come. And maybe we was. But I'm glad we did. How you feeling, Gray?'

'I'm feeling much better. And I'm not sleepy.'

'Aren't you? Well, I am. So just you lie quiet and get your strength back.'

'Yes, Lynn.'

'We got plenty of time.'

'Yes, Lynn. The rest of our lives.'

'That's right, pet. Let's hope so, anyway. Good-night, Prof, love. God bless.'

Chapter Ten

– Up to the surface, slowly, slowly to the surface. Don't want to wake, must wake. Wake up, wake up. What the –?

– It's not happening.

– It *is* happening. Her head on the pillow. She's fast asleep, dead to the world. Snoring gently. Like a cat's purr.

– Hey! Graham Hollis! You left home! With her! The enormity of it. The madness of it.

– I know. It's mad. But.

– They'll be after you. They'll know by now. They'll have been up all night. Ringing the police every half hour.

– Oh God. Yes. Oh God.

– They'll be hunting now. Police alerted. Walkie-talkies. Missing from home in Crimley, Graham Hollis, sixteen, tall, slim, fair, may be wearing dark green anorak. Believed to be in company of blonde girl . . .

– Steady on. Not all *that* unusual. Not at my age. No nationwide search. Not like child missing on way home from school.

– They'll put out description, though. Tell police everywhere.

– Will they? Don't know what they do. *She* might know. She's not worried, anyway. Still fast asleep.

– They're hunting for you. You're hunted. Wanted. Hunted. Wanted.

– They don't know where to look. They'll have

asked at Crimley station. We'll be remembered there. Were there for an hour, inquiring about London. That's where young couples go, running away. London. They won't think of Pool-on-Sea. We laid a false trail. Pretty smart.

— What about Charlie? In the little grey van?

— He doesn't know much. And why should he care?

— Go back, boy! Go back!

— Can't. Too late.

— Can. Sneak away, get early train. Small escapade, soon forgotten. Say you were upset, all finished now, nothing happened.

— What do you mean, nothing happened?

— You know. They know. Nothing *has* happened. Yet. Get out while you can.

— I can't. Won't. I love her. *Love* her.

— You're nervous, you know you are. Scared stiff. And so you should be. A missing person. Hunted.

— They won't look for us here.

— Hunted. What about Uncle Roger, Aunt Josie, a few streets away? Get home, quick. Or else.

— Or else. Calm down, calm down. Or else what? Or else go right ahead, no panic, get to Scotland, live there a week or two, get married, and then they can't part us. Safe, married, in love for ever. No problem. We ought to be on our way, though. What time? Nearly nine o'clock. Later than I thought. Hungry. Stomach all right now, but empty. Get some breakfast. Eight till nine, the notice said. Better wake her up. Gently, gently. Just a touch. No effect. Kiss her awake. Go on, don't be frightened, kiss her . . . Some sleeper.

Her hand moved across her face, brushing him away.

'What is it? What's up?'

'Morning, Lynn.'

'Bugger off.'

She turned over, drew up the sheets.

'Lynn! Time for breakfast!'

'What?'

'Breakfast!'

'I don't eat bloody breakfast.'

'Well, I'll go, Lynn, if you don't mind. I'm hungry after yesterday.'

'Go on, then. Don't make a speech about it.'

Graham dressed. As he went out she said:

'Bring me a cup of tea back.'

'I'll ring for some if you like, Lynn.'

'Ring for it? In a place like this? Don't be so daft. Bring a cup back with you.'

She stirred, and peered over the sheets.

'Did you bring me that cup of tea?'

'They wouldn't let me.'

'They what?'

'I asked the woman, and she said what would they do if everybody started taking cups to the bedrooms and leaving them around.'

'Well, you silly – oh, never mind. You don't *ask*, you just take it while nobody's looking.'

'Sorry, Lynn.'

'I could just have done with that cup of tea.'

'Sorry, Lynn. Is there anything else I can do?'

'Yes. You can go and get me some fags. Ten Embassy. Go on. Don't start kissing me now, I'm not in the mood.'

God, what a day. Cold, wet, windy. Blowing in from the sea. Button up your collar. Still people around on holiday. Fancy being on holiday in this.

Ten Embassy. Where to get ten Embassy? Not in this street, anyway. Nothing here but cheap hotels, boarding-houses.

– It's not happening.

– Oh yes it is. Ten Embassy, that's what's happening. Round the corner and on to the front. Get them at that kiosk near the pier entrance. What a day. Cold, wet, windy, blowing in from the sea.

– Look out! A policeman!

– So what, a policeman?

– Missing person. Hunted.

– Don't be daft. He doesn't know me from Adam.

– All forces alerted. Walkie-talkies. Missing, boy aged sixteen, tall . . .

– He can't know who I am. One person in fifty million. Not all *that* important. No need to feel so guilty. Nothing to worry about.

– Why's your heart thumping, then?

– Just silliness. Look, he's gone past. I knew he would.

– Nasty moment, though. Plenty more ahead.

– Nonsense. Have to stop imagining things. Roll on Scotland, marriage, safety.

– Marriage? You saw her this morning. Fancy that every day.

– Plenty of people are bad-tempered when they wake up.

– Abusive.

– I love her.

– Common.

– I love her.

– Kiosk's open, anyway. Newspapers, sweets, cigarettes.

'Ten Embassy, please . . . Thank you.'

'Hey, son, what about your change?'

'Oh, thank you, I forgot.'

– Careful, that's suspicious.

– Don't be silly. 'Course it's not suspicious. People forget their change every day. And in this wind and rain, nobody lingers. Talk about cold and wet! No day for a walk on the promenade. They *are* walking on the promenade, though. Like the man over there with the red setter, the one that looks a bit like Uncle Roger's Sandy.

– Sandy! That *is* Sandy!

– I don't think so. Long way off. Just another red setter.

– And the man coming up behind. It's Uncle Roger!

– Can't tell from here.

– It's his build. And look, he's waving!

– Not to me.

– Yes. To you!

– Double back! Into the side-street, quick! Nowhere to hide. Run along, right to the end. A doorway at last, thank goodness. Peep out. Man's going past.

– He looked this way.

– He didn't.

– He did. It was Uncle Roger.

– Wasn't.

– And Sandy.

– No. Just a red setter, one of hundreds.

– Heading for police-station.

– No. Going for a walk. Past police-station, that's coincidence.

– It was him. He saw you. Waved to you.

– Rubbish. Just a man with a dog. Can't go on in this state. Have to get a grip. Calm down, take it easy, walk gently back to hotel, unconcerned. Breathe deeply, relax, all's well.

– What if it *was* him, though? Telling police?

'Hullo, Gray.'

'Hullo, Lynn. I brought your cigarettes. Lynn, listen. I think we . . .'

'Thank you, love. You're a pet. Sorry I bit your head off. I'm *like* that in the morning. I keep trying not to be, but it doesn't seem to make no difference.'

'It doesn't matter. Lynn, I think we should get away from here.'

'Okay, love. No hurry, though. Sit down and talk to me.'

'I thought I saw my Uncle Roger.'

'Did you? Gray, love, your clothes is wet. Take them off.'

'My Uncle Roger. He was walking on the promenade with his dog.'

'Was he, now?'

'Yes, Lynn. And I thought *he* saw *me*.'

'Never mind what *he* saw, pet. You look at *me*. Am I nice?'

'Oh, Lynn, yes, you're lovely, but what I'm trying to say is this. If my uncle saw me he might be telephoning my parents or telling the police or something. So I think we ought to leave here right away.'

'Did he see which way you went?'

'I don't think so. No I'm sure he didn't. But –'

'So he won't be round here in five minutes' time bashing the door down?'

'No. But –'

'Never mind him, then, that's what I say. Gray, love, don't *worry* so. I want you to be happy, see You can't start too soon.'

'But Lynn –'

'There, you just come to me and take it easy. I love you, Gray. I never said that to a fellow before, not in my life. I love you truly. I'm going to *show* you I love you.'

'Lynn, no. We've got to go, now.'

'Gray. Yes.'

'No. Not yet.'

'Oh, for crying out loud, Prof, are you a man or a flipping mouse? There's plenty that'd be glad to be where you are now, I can tell you.'

'I know, Lynn. But don't you see. I'm frightened of something coming between us. I'd rather not have anything at all than that. I want us to be married and have all our lives together.'

'There's something about you, Prof, that's not natural.'

'Lynn, it's not true. I do love you, I do want you. But I'd like to get away from Pool-on-Sea. Will you come? Please?'

'Oh, go to hell.'

'We could get to Edinburgh today, Lynn. Then I'd feel safe. We could give notice to get married, or whatever you have to do.'

' 'S a long way to Edinburgh. And pouring with rain. I'm not going out hitching in that.'

'We could go by train. Change at Cobchester. That'd be the best way, and quickest. I've still got nearly all my money. I don't mind spending a bit. It's worth it, to get us there.'

'I never been to Scotland. I don't know that I want to.'

'But Lynn, that was the whole idea. You said you'd come. You said you'd marry me. You said you loved me, only five minutes ago.'

'Five minutes ago is five minutes ago. Listen, Prof, if I hadn't been fed up with Jeff I wouldn't have looked twice at you. And listen again. If I get married, I'll marry a fellow what takes a proper interest in a girl. Somebody what's got blood in his flipping veins, not milk and water.'

'Lynn, I do –'

'Fancy me, sitting here in my flipping nightie, arguing. *That's* fun, isn't it, I don't think. Just you flip off home to your mummy and daddy, and don't take up no more of my time.'

'All right, if that's how you feel.'

'It *is* how I feel. Pack your flipping bag and get out.'

'And what will *you* do, Lynn?'

'I might get a job here. Plenty of jobs at Pool-on-Sea. What's it to do with you, anyway?'

'Don't go back to Crimley.'

'I will if I want. And I won't if I don't want. Mind your own business . . . You afraid I might say hullo to you in the street while you're with your parents or something?'

'I wasn't thinking of that at all.'

'P'raps you'd like me to give you a certificate to take home with you. Dear Mr and Mrs Thing, this is to certify that your son is still a virgin. And likely to remain so.'

'Oh, Lynn, don't. And don't send me away, I can't bear it.'

'Don't weep on *my* flipping shoulder, mate. Go on, hop it before I get dressed, I'm not putting on a show for you.'

'I shan't go back to my parents, Lynn.'

'You will.'

'No, I won't. I don't know what I'll do. I don't want to live without you. I'll – I'll go up Pool Tower and jump off!'

'You know damn well you won't.'

'I'll do *something* drastic. I'll never go back to Crimley. Even if I don't kill myself, it's the end of everything that matters. I won't have anything to care about.'

'Here, take this, then, you great drip!'

She threw the toy dog at him.

'Lynn!'

'What, you again? I thought you'd gone ten minutes ago.'

'Lynn, I'm sorry. I *was* a great drip.'

'Did you come back to tell me that?'

'I was upset, I went all to pieces.'

'You can say that again.'

'I'm learning my lesson, though. I just made a resolution, Lynn. I'm going to grow up.'

'That's interesting. When? This year, next year?'

'As quick as I can. Starting today. Lynn, have I really lost you?'

'I didn't know I was yours to lose.'

'I mean, is this the end?'

'Reckon so. I told you, go home and be good.'

'I won't go back, Lynn. I did mean that. I won't go back, ever. I guess I'll find a job and grow up by working. And – well, if we're finished, all I can do is wish you well.'

He put out his hand.

Then she had her arms round him and was laughing helplessly.

'What are you laughing at?' he asked.

'Oh, Prof, you were so *noble!*'

'I don't see what's funny about it.'

'Don't you? I do. Graham, pet, I'm glad you came back. You're so lovely sometimes it just isn't true. I don't know how I had the heart to send you packing. You looked so pathetic when you went out, just like poor little Butch if *he'd* had a telling-off. And it was as much my fault as yours. You don't understand women, pet, that's the trouble. I guess you got a lot to learn. Still, you *will* learn plenty before we're through.'

'We're not going to be through, Lynn. Ever.'

'All right, love. That was a nice snap in your voice. Decisive, sort of. Have you started growing up already?'

'You're laughing at me again.'

'I'm not, pet, honestly. Now, what's all this panic about seeing your uncle? Are you *sure* it was him?'

'No, Lynn, I'm not sure. And if it was, I'm not sure he saw me. And he might not know I've left home anyway. It's just the feeling of it. You understand? I don't feel right. As if we're too near to home and people that know us. I want to be a long way off.'

'In Scotland, eh?'

'Yes.'

'Young Lockupshop or whatever his name was.'

'Yes. Fair Ellen. Fair Lynn.'

'Oh well, pet, if you feel you got to get away, we'll get away. It's all experience, I reckon. Sounds as if it's still pouring down, though. We'll go by train, like you said. Here, let's be devils, let's do it in style. They got a phone here, Gray. Ring for a taxi to the station.'

'Gray.'

'Yes, Lynn.'

'It's a long way to Edinburgh.'

'Yes, it is, Lynn. Well, we don't have to stay there after we're married. We can live where we like. But we do have to go to Scotland first.'

'I know, Gray. Takes a bit of getting used to, that's all. Look, do we have to do it all today? We got to change trains at Cobchester, you said. I got a girl-friend at Cobchester. Betty her name is. She's married. I'd like to see her again. Listen, Gray, they got a good big council flat, and there's only two of them and the baby. We could stay there, pet.'

'How long for?'

'Just for a night or two. Over the week-end, maybe, and then on to Edinburgh on Monday. We can't do anything about getting married before Monday, can we?'

'I suppose not. But –'

'And it'd be ever so late by the time we got there, wouldn't it? That's if we could do it one day at all.'

'Well, yes. But –'

'And we'll be safe in Cobchester, pet. Cobchester's big, and no one'll be looking for us there.'

'No, but –'

'You got a better idea, Gray?'

'No, but –'

'Leave it to me, then. We'll be all right. Just get two one-way tickets to Cobchester.'

Chapter Eleven

'Ring again, Gray.'

'No good, Lynn. Nobody's coming.'

'Betty might have gone to the shops, seeing it's Sat'day afternoon. We'll go for a cup of tea, then come back later. Oh, wait a minute, Gray, I can hear footsteps. There's somebody at home after all. Here they come. Hullo, Tim. How are you? This is Graham Hollis, friend of mine.'

'What you want, Lynn?'

'Came to see Betty, that's all.'

'She's not here.'

'When'll she be back, Tim?'

'What you want her for?'

'We're old pals, Tim, you know that. I used to play with Betty when I was a kid, before I went to Birmingham. When we both lived round the corner in Orchid Grove. Those were the days. It hasn't half changed, Tim, hasn't it?'

'I said, what you want, Lynn?'

'Well, me and my friend – my fiancé, I mean – we was thinking you might put us up for a night or two before we move on.'

'Nothing doing.'

'It's not for long, Tim. Not permanent. We're on a business trip. To London or Scotland or somewhere.'

'Nothing doing.'

'We weren't just trying to save a pound or two. I

wanted to see Betty. It's over a year since I saw her. You was only just married.'

'I told you, Betty's not here.'

A voice came from behind.

'Who is it, Tim?'

'Nobody.'

'Betty!' Lynn shouted. 'It's me. Lynn!'

Tim stepped forward, closed the door behind him. He was a burly man who hadn't shaved for a day or two.

'For the last time, Lynn,' he said. 'You're not seeing her. Hop it. *And* your pal.' He moved forward. 'Quick!'

Lynn rolled her eyes.

'Come on, Gray,' she said. 'We're not staying where we're not wanted.'

Graham followed her down the staircase of the apartment block.

'I felt uneasy when I had to turn my back on him,' he said. 'As if I might feel a boot behind me.'

'Yes. And you might have done, too. He's nasty, is Tim Ridgeway, when he's that way out. Sorry, pet.' She sighed. 'That's marriage for you.'

'What do you mean, Lynn, "that's marriage"?'

'She married him, see, love? And what can you do then? She has a kiddy, and I dare say another on the way by now, and she's helpless. Signed her life away. I seen it happen before.'

'But not often, Lynn, surely. Not nowadays.'

'You'd be surprised, pet. Fellows that seem keen enough to please before they get married, they change afterwards so much you wouldn't know them. They get the power, see, and then they start using it. And if you've a kiddy, or two or three, they got you just where they want you. You don't know *anything*, Prof. You don't know what life's about. You don't know you're born.'

'It just doesn't sound like our world, Lynn.'

'It may not sound like yours. It sounds like mine. And maybe it's more like yours than you think, pet. Things change on the surface, they don't change all that much underneath. Old Mother Nature's the same as she always was. There's just one way you can beat the old cow these days if you're a woman, and that's by not having kids. That's why I'm careful. No patter of tiny feet for me, thank you.'

'You don't think *I'd* try to chain a person up, do you?'

'No, pet, 'course I don't.'

'I'll play fair with you every way I can, Lynn. Always.'

'Always is a long time, Gray.'

'Don't you trust me?'

'There, there, am I hurting your feelings again? I only mean that life's a funny thing and there's no telling what'll happen. But yes, I do trust you, Gray. You're kind, you got imagination. You'll be lovely to the girl you marry.'

'Which is you. So do as you're always telling me to do, and stop worrying. We're going to be happy ever after. Look, Lynn, it's stopped raining and the sun's coming out and we're together and everything's lovely.'

'Bless you, Prof. I'm all right now. I was a bit upset, thinking about Betty, that's all. We were kids together around here, you know. It didn't look like it does now, though. All these blocks of flats is new. They pulled the old houses down. We used to call it the Jungle, I don't know why. See that stretch of water? That's the North-west Junction Canal. And those cottages on the edge of it, down by the viaduct?

I remember those. They must be all that's left of the old Jungle.'

'We'd better be on our way, Lynn. Back to the station and see how soon we can get a train north.'

'Could do, Gray. It's getting a bit late, though. Past four o'clock.'

'You'd rather stay in Cobchester tonight, wouldn't you, Lynn? You still haven't quite got used to the thought of Edinburgh.'

'That's right, Prof. You *are* learning about me, aren't you? I didn't think you understood.'

'I can understand just a little bit, Lynn. Particularly when it's somebody I love.'

'All right. Well, understand a bit more and don't get soppy, see . . . I keep thinking about that place down by the viaduct, Gray. We used to go there sometimes when we were kids, just two or three of us. There was a kind of den over the top of the cottages. We used to play there for hours . . . Here, Gray, I just had an idea. Come over and have a look.'

They crossed a bare cindery space to the row of small houses on the canal bank.

'Looks a bit depressing, doesn't it?' Graham said. 'All empty and derelict. Even in this sunshine.'

'Yes. But now, come round the side, love. See that door up there in the gable end, opening on to nothing at all? That's where the den used to be, over the top of all four cottages. We used to love being up there, playing house. Can you climb, Graham?'

'Hey, Lynn, what are you getting at?'

'There's two or three missing bricks that'd help you to shin up that drain-pipe. Then see if you can open the window. It's a flipping miracle that window's not broken. Maybe somebody's lived here recently. Could be. That's right, Gray, up you go.

Now, push the window up, if it still moves. Hurray, you're in. What's it like in there?'

Graham put his head out of the window.

'Not bad,' he said. 'Drier than you'd expect.'

'It always was dry. Got a good roof on it.'

'And what do you know, Lynn? There's a ladder in here.'

'Another flipping miracle. Fancy it not being pinched. You'd think it was *meant* for us, wouldn't you? Now, take a look at the floor. Notice anything?'

'Yes, Lynn. There's a trapdoor.'

'That's right. Open it, pet. Push that ladder down.'

Graham manoeuvred the ladder through the trapdoor. By the time he had the lower end of it on the floor of the cottage below, Lynn was waiting there. She climbed the ladder and stood beside him.

They were in a long, narrow attic, high in the middle, sloping at the sides, with three grimy windows. There was an ancient bedstead with mattress and pile of grey Army blankets. There was a deal table, there were two or three pieces of battered ugly furniture and a paraffin lamp and heater. Dust lay on everything.

'Well,' said Lynn. 'I don't know about you, pet, but I've slept in worse places than this. Much worse.'

'Lynn! You weren't thinking –?'

' 'Course I was, love. And still am. Just the place for a quiet weekend.'

'Hullo, Lynn. Here I am.'

'Hullo, Gray, love. So you are. You were a long time, though, weren't you?'

'I had to wait at the fish-and-chip shop. They ran out just before I got served. But these are from the new batch. They're nice and fresh.'

'You brought plenty, pet. That's good. I got quite an appetite again.'

'Lynn, you've made a difference to the place, haven't you? It looks like home, now.'

'Well. Sort of. To tell you the truth, Gray, I'm not a great one for housework and all that. So don't get the wrong idea. But I thought we could do without all that dust.'

'And you got the paraffin heater going!'

'Yes, pet. Never thought it'd work. It smelt a bit at first. But you can't smell it now, can you?'

'No. Well, not much.'

'I reckon someone was living here until a few months ago, and left, sudden. Dunno who he was, but we owe him a vote of thanks. He left us all we needed. Like a broom, that I swept the floor with. And some socks and shirts, that I used for dusting. And a can of paraffin for the lamp and the heater. And a couple of plates, that we're eating off now. And two cups, that you can pour that orange drink into, and hurry up, I'm thirsty.'

'And did he leave the transistor?'

'No, that's mine. I shoved it in the bottom of my bag when I left Jeff's, and didn't think about it till just now. It cheers things up, doesn't it?'

'Yes, Lynn. Maybe we should turn it down, though. We don't want to attract attention, do we?'

'Guess not, pet. That better?'

'That's fine.'

'Funny how memories come back, Gray. I'd forgot about this place for years. But I remember it quite well now. There was four of us that used to play here. Me and Betty and the two Thompson kids, Harold and Jean. Harold was a year or two older. He was a bright little lad. Somebody told me he finished up at Oxford University. Makes you think, doesn't it? Here, Gray, aren't you going to finish them chips?'

'I've had enough, Lynn.'

'I'll eat them . . . You know, Gray, young Harold didn't have *any* advantages, his family were a real rough lot. Now as for you, you got everything. You oughtn't to be throwing it all away, ought you? Not really.'

'Don't say things like that, Lynn. I know what I'm doing.'

'I hope you do, love.'

'I know very well. I know better and better all the time. I love you, Lynn. I care more about you than I do about advantages. And anyway I'm not all that clever. And even if I was, it wouldn't make any difference. I'm happy, Lynn. Are you?'

'Mmmm. Those fish and chips were good, pet. I was ready for them. I feel nice and comfortable now. And this place has got something, hasn't it? Feels like home, doesn't it? . . . Are you warm enough, Gray?'

'Warm as toast. But I've been wondering if *you* were warm enough, like that.'

'Oh. So you did notice, then?'

'I could hardly *not* notice, could I, Lynn? You changed while I was out. You're wearing your nightie under that jacket.'

'You noticed but you didn't say anything.'

'I thought we'd better eat. While the food was hot.'

'That's a good boy. First things first . . . You're blushing again.'

'I'm sorry, Lynn, I can't help it.'

'Don't apologize, pet, it's sweet. Now, you never told me this morning, do you like my nightie?'

'Yes, Lynn, very much.'

' 'S pretty, isn't it?'

'Yes. Very.'

'And me?'

'Oh, Lynn, yes, yes, yes.'

'You're trembling, love. That won't do. It's a good job you've got me to look after you. Easy now, don't think about yourself, just be natural. This isn't one of your flipping exams. Don't worry, Graham, you haven't a care in the world. Not at this minute, you haven't. Not a care in the world.'

'Don't keep apologizing, pet. There's no call for it.'

'I wasn't very good, Lynn.'

' 'Course you weren't. What do you expect? You can't do everything right first time.'

'I thought I might have done better, all the same.'

'You weren't so bad, Gray. Honest. You'll be all right. Being shy doesn't help you, but that'll wear off, you'll be surprised how soon.'

'I didn't mean it to be like this, Lynn. I meant us to be married first. You know that, don't you?'

'I should think so, pet. You said it often enough.'

'I didn't go off with you just for a – bit of fun.'

'What's wrong with a bit of fun? Aren't you due for some?'

'Lynn, you're still wearing your wedding-ring from the market.'

'So I am, pet.'

'I want to buy you a real one, like I told you. But till I do, will you wear this one for me, Lynn?'

'What d'you mean, Gray?'

'Well – look, give it me. Let me put it on your finger. With this ring I –'

'No, Gray, no!'

'Why not, Lynn?'

'No, I tell you! Don't do that!'

'Is it because I – wasn't much good?'

' 'S not that at all, pet. You've nothing to worry about. But I don't like the wedding-ring business. It bothers me, it doesn't feel right.'

'It feels right to me.'

'Graham, love, you *still* got an awful lot to learn. Now, just settle down and rest. Quite dark now, isn't it? It's not late, but I feel like we've had a busy day. Does it seem years to you since we was at Pool-on-Sea?'

'Years and years. So much has happened since then. *Everything's* happened since then.'

'You lost that certificate I was going to give you, Gray. Do you feel different?'

'Not as different as I thought I would. But I love you even more, Lynn. You were nice just now. You might have laughed at me.'

'I wouldn't do that to anyone. It's a bitch's trick . . . Still warm enough, Gray?'

'Plenty warm enough. Are you?'

'Fine. It's a bit cramped, and these blankets is rough. But *you're* nice, Gray. You're nice to be with.'

'Lynn! I'd almost forgotten. They'll still be looking for us!'

'They won't find us here, pet. Now, honestly, how could they? It's the end of the world. But just for now it's home and it's safe. And I'm not going to let you worry any more. So snuggle down. Good-night, Prof, love. God bless.'

Chapter Twelve

'Gray.'

'Yes, Lynn.'

'Why aren't you asleep?'

'Why aren't *you*?'

'Dunno, I was just thinking.'

'What about, Lynn?'

'Oh, about us. And your mum and dad. What was *you* thinking about, Gray?'

'We're on the run, Lynn. It still scares me. Sets my heart thumping.'

'You got to see it the size it really is, pet. I'm eighteen, I'm of age. You're nearly seventeen. We're not the first couple that's ever gone missing. The police aren't going to waste much manpower on *us*, I can tell you that.'

'But my parents. And Jeff. What if Jeff's after you?'

'I'm not worrying about Jeff. Maybe he wants me back, maybe he doesn't. But if you think he's going to leave the business to look after itself while he hunts the country for me, like a needle in a flipping haystack, you don't know Jeff. Now your parents, that's another matter. But it seems to me they just got no way of finding us. There's only two ways they're going to see you again in the next two or three weeks, Gray. One's if you was to go back of your own accord.'

'I won't do that.'

'The other's if somebody was to give you away.'

'But who, Lynn, who?'

'I dunno. I was only saying what *could* happen.'

'But Lynn, you've said yourself, nobody knows where we are, nobody. So how could anyone give us away?'

'I don't know, pet. I don't know.'

'I'm surprised you should think about it.'

'I guess you can never rule things out, pet. Same as I don't rule it out that you'd go back of your own accord.'

'That's not nice, Lynn. I've told you I won't.'

'I know, Gray. But you're thoughtful, more than what I am. Now as for me, I just put things behind me and forget about them. And I never cared about anybody much. Why should I? – a fat lot anyone ever cared about *me*. But *you*, Gray, you think and you care. And I reckon before long you're going to start thinking about your mum and dad and wondering whether you was right to start on all this. Specially now that you – now that you've lost that certificate.'

'That's not nice, either.'

'I can't help it, Prof. Maybe I'm *not* nice. Maybe that's another thing. Maybe it's just a girl you wanted, any girl, not specially me.'

'I could nearly hate you for saying that.'

'I'm sorry, love. I wouldn't like it to be true. But are you sure it couldn't be? Absolutely sure?'

'Yes, I'm sure, Lynn. I love you. For being who you are. Not just for – you know. You believe me, Lynn, don't you? You have to believe me.'

'All right, pet. I believe you. But Prof, even if you know what you want, are you sure you know what's best for you?'

'What was that, Lynn? What did you say? I didn't quite catch it.'

'Nothing, pet.'

'Gray.'

'Yes, Lynn.'

'Why aren't you asleep *still*?'

'Just thinking.'

'About *them*.'

'Yes, Lynn. How did you know?'

'You heard me tell that fellow that gave us the ride to Pool, I got second sight. It's true, Gray, sort of. I knew he was married and had kids. He never told me, I didn't have any clues, I just knew. And I knew you was thinking about your mum and dad.'

'It was you that put it into my mind, Lynn.'

'No, I didn't. It was there already. How'll they be taking it, Gray?'

'Badly. My mother'll be in hysterics, I dare say. My dad'll be calmer, but he'll feel it just as much. I guess I'm all they have, Lynn. It'll be like their world coming down round their ears.'

'And if you go back in three weeks' time and say, "Hullo, Mum and Dad, I'm married, here she is," will that bring them round?'

'Well –'

'It won't, will it?'

'Maybe not altogether. But they'll have to get used to it.'

'Even if they did, your mum'd never stop hating me. For being another woman that had taken her blue-eyed boy away from her, to say nothing of thinking I was a bit of dirt you'd picked up in the gutter. Your dad – well, I don't know. He'd tell me to take speech training and join the tennis club. It wouldn't do, Gray. Honest, now, would it?'

'If it'd do for you, it'd do for me.'

'But would you be happy, Gray, feeling you'd – what was it you said? – brought their flipping world round their ears?'

'Here, Lynn, whose side are you on?'

'Yours, pet. Don't get me wrong. I'm not the forgiving type. Not after the way they made me feel. To hell with them, that's what I say. But you, Gray, you got the rest of your life ahead of you. That's what's worrying me.'

'You keep telling *me* not to worry. Now *you* stop worrying, Lynn. Do as you're told and go to sleep.'

'Okay, Prof. If that's what you say. Good-night, Prof, love.'

'Good-night, Lynn, love. God bless.'

– Church clock somewhere, striking. Trains rumble over viaduct. Hard mattress. She's got the blankets. No peace.

– Seems to be striking thirteen. No, only twelve. That's better. Feels later than it is. Been here for ever. In an attic, somewhere in Cobchester. With her. That cat's-purr of a snore. A delicate snore. Sounds daft, a delicate snore.

– *She's* fast asleep, anyway.

– So what? Hasn't she a right to be?

– Whatever she says about worrying, it isn't keeping *her* awake like it is you.

– Not just worry. Church clock, trains, hard bed.

– Think of *them*. That's the heart of the matter. Taken you long enough to reach it. Think of them.

– Haven't *I* any rights? Hasn't she?

– They only have you. Bringing their world round their ears.

– They stifled me. Now I can breathe.

– They love you. All these years. Done everything for you. What return?

– Not my fault I was born. Didn't ask.

– Paid fees, clothes, holidays. They love you.

– She loves me, too.

– How long for? Today, tomorrow, next week. Then someone else.

– And I love her.

– Just a bit of stuff, that's all.

– No.

– You got what you wanted.

– No, no.

– Wasn't all that wonderful, either.

– Shut up.

– Be sensible. Call it off.

– No.

– Rest of your life ahead. Good home, good prospects. Hang on to them.

– No.

– Fine profession, gives you a place in the world. Grow up, learn to value it. Leave her while you can.

– No.

Sunshine through a grimy window.

'Graham.'

'Huh? What?'

'Graham. Graham.'

'Hullo, Lynn.'

'I thought you'd never wake up, Gray.'

'Seems the wrong way round, Lynn. I feel as if I'm the one that should be awake while you sleep on.'

'I admit I like my beauty sleep, pet. But I reckon I've had it this time. About twelve hours of it. It's past ten o'clock, Gray. And it looks a lovely day out there. How you feeling? Full of energy?'

'Not bad, Lynn. Not bad at all. How are you?'

'I'm fine, pet. What about a nice healthy walk in the fresh air?'

'What, this minute? Lynn, you're teasing.'

'Who says I'm teasing?'

'I say you're teasing.'

'Well . . . All right, maybe I'm teasing. It *is* quite nice and cosy inside. I like this place, don't you, Gray? You couldn't call it posh, but it does feel more and more like home.'

'It's because we're together. *Anywhere'd* be nice with you. And listen, Lynn. I thought it all out. I thought about it for hours. I know just how much it'll hurt my mum and dad, but we've got our lives to live too, and we've more life ahead of us than they have. I weighed it all up and I reckon the balance comes down on our side. And I decided. Definitely. Finally. I'm not going back.'

'I see, pet. And what if – what if something was to happen to me?'

'What sort of something? What could happen?'

'Well – say I was to step under a bus. Or lose my memory and wander off.'

'You won't step under a bus. And you'd better not lose your memory.'

'Or suppose – suppose we was to have a row and I was to get cross with you and go?'

'Lynn, if you walked out on me, I'd chase you to the ends of the earth and bring you back. But even if I didn't find you I'd not go home to Crimley. Because you've freed me from it, and I'm staying free.'

'That's what you feel now, Gray. You might not feel it always.'

'Oh yes I will. Always. I've made up my mind. But Lynn, I'm not having this talk about walking out on me. You're not to do any such thing. Promise me you won't.'

'Now, now, Prof, you're getting too bossy. You haven't the right to ask for a promise like that.'

'I don't care whether I've the right or not. I *am* asking for it. I'll give you the same promise, Lynn. I won't walk out on you whatever happens. Now you promise me. Promise faithfully.'

'All right, Gray. I promise. I won't walk out on you.'

'Oh Lynn, it's marvellous to be certain. I'm ten feet tall today, I'm so happy it just isn't true. Lynn, come here!'

'What, aren't I close enough?'

'No.'

'Hey, Prof!'

'Don't call me that today, Lynn. I don't feel like the poor little prof you thought I was last week.'

'No, I can see you don't.'

'Oh Lynn, you're so wonderful I can't bear it. And if you stuck a knife into me you'd find I *have* got blood inside. The red stuff. Not milk and water.'

'I believe you, pet . . . Here, you're supposed to be shy.'

'You said I'd get over it.'

'You're getting over it pretty quick. Aren't you, Gray? You're a bad boy. What would they think of you now?'

'I don't care what they'd think about me now. I only care about you.'

'Here, Gray, I aren't half thirsty, are you?'

'There's some of that orange stuff left in the bottle. Coming over.'

'Mmmm. That was good. There's nothing like a nice fresh drink when you're thirsty. Want a swig, Gray?'

'Yes, please, Lynn.'

'Leave another drop for me.'

'There, now, you finish it off. I guess that's our breakfast, Lynn.'

'Yes, pet. 'S enough for me. I never feel like eating in the morning.'

'I like a good hot breakfast as a rule, Lynn. But today I couldn't care less. Shall I tell you something? This is the nicest breakfast I ever had in my life. Drinking orange stuff out of the same bottle with you. In fact it's the happiest day of my life.'

'Good for you, pet.'

'And think of all the happy days to come! I feel on top of the world, Lynn. Look at that patch of sunlight moving down the wall. It'll be on *us* in a minute. I suppose in this attic we *are* on top of the world. Nothing above us but a few slates. Next stop, heaven. And we're going to be married, Lynn. Married! . . . They won't catch us, will they, Lynn? Nobody could give us away. They couldn't, could they?'

'Well – you can't be too sure, love.'

'What do you mean, Lynn? How could anyone catch us? You said yourself the police wouldn't try too hard. Who *could* give us away?'

'I – oh, I don't know.'

'Don't frighten me, Lynn. It was such a funny look you gave me then.'

'Oh, Gray, you keep reminding me of poor little Butch. He had just the same expression. And sometimes if there was big dogs around he'd sort of puff himself up as if he was saying, "I'm a big dog, too," but he was only the same little Butch. He got run over in the end. By a butcher's van . . . I don't like to think of *you* getting hurt, Gray.'

'Then don't think of it. Think of nice things, like Edinburgh.'

'Folk do get hurt, all the same.'

'What do you mean, Lynn? You're frightening me again. There's only one way I could get hurt.'

'There's a hundred ways, Prof. You don't know. You're like my Butch, you're only little.'

'What d'you mean, only little? I'm six foot two. How tall are you?'

'I'm five foot six.'

'Who's little, then?'

'You know what I mean, Gray. You're a kid. I'm years older than you. Centuries. Now, lie down and relax. Go on being happy for a bit.'

'I don't want to be happy just for a bit, Lynn. I want to be happy for a lifetime. Do you want me to be happy for a lifetime, Lynn?'

'Yes, pet.'

'You know what to do, then.'

'Yes, pet.'

'Gray.'

'Yes, Lynn.'

'Are you hungry?'

'Well. Since you mention it, yes, Lynn.'

'I'm famished, Gray. I could eat that flipping horse again.'

'It's a good job we're in the twentieth century, or running off with you'd cost a fortune in horses.'

'I'd like to go out for a meal, pet.'

'Why not another picnic? In here, nice and cosy, or outside in the sun. You choose.'

'I'd rather eat out. In a restaurant.'

'That means being with other people. A picnic's just us. I'd prefer it to be just us.'

'It's Sunday, you know, Gray.'

'Yes. Still, I expect we can buy some food somewhere. I'll go, Lynn. I'll be as quick as I can.'

'I'd rather go out for a meal, Gray. I would, really. Somewhere nice.'

'All right, Lynn. If that's what you want. Lynn,

is anything the matter? You've got that funny look again. As if you'd been thinking.'

'Even *I* think sometimes, pet. Not often, but sometimes. In a simple kind of way.'

'You're not simple, Lynn.'

'You don't know *what* I am.'

'I know you've been thinking something you don't want to tell me. And I'm worried.'

'And I'm tired of telling you, don't *worry* so. Now, come on, Prof, put some clothes on, let's go.'

'Where shall we go, then?'

'Listen, Gray. You said this was the happiest day of your life, right? Well, let's celebrate. I got a good idea. Let's go to the Royal Britannia.'

'That great big hotel we saw opposite the station?'

'That's it, pet.'

'But Lynn, we can't. It'd cost a fortune.'

'My treat, Gray. I told you before, I got money. Jeff owed me four weeks' wages and I flipping well took it.'

'I don't want to spend your money, Lynn.'

'That's what money's for, pet.'

'Anyway, I think we should be careful. We might have to pay rent in advance when we get to Edinburgh, and we don't know how long it'll take us to get jobs. Or how soon we'll get any wages.'

'We'll be careful with *your* money, pet, but I'm not going to be careful with mine. I want to treat you, Graham. I won't take no for an answer.'

'Won't we be a bit conspicuous in a big hotel?'

'A bit what?'

'Conspicuous. Noticeable. I mean, when all's said and done, there's people looking for us, or there may be. And a place like that isn't exactly private.'

'I can't see that they'll be looking for us any more in the Royal Britannia than anywhere else.'

'I suppose not, Lynn. It still seems a funny place to go, though. And anyway, we're not smart enough, or at least I'm not. I can't go into the best hotel in town wearing an old anorak.'

'You're all right in the grill-room, Gray. So long as you're clean and decent, that's all they ask in the grill-room. And sober, of course.'

'You seem to know all about it, Lynn.'

'I'm in my home town, remember.'

'There must be plenty of people around who're in their home town, but they don't all know what you have to wear in the Royal Britannia Hotel.'

'What you getting at, Gray?'

'You used to come to Cobchester with Jeff, didn't you?'

'Now listen, Prof. You know I used to be with Jeff, you've known it all along. What I did then isn't your business. How long have you known me?'

'Nine days, Lynn.'

'I been around a long time before that. And done a lot that you haven't heard of.'

'I know, Lynn. I'm sorry I mentioned Jeff. I don't care what you've done before. I'm only bothered about what we're doing now.'

'There, pet, don't get upset. I'll tell you what we're doing. We're going out for a lovely meal and I'm paying.'

'And after that, Lynn? What are we doing after that?'

'I don't know what we're doing after that.'

'Well, I'll tell you, then. We're coming back

here, and we're going to bed early, and first thing tomorrow morning we'll be on our way to Scotland. All right?'

'All right, pet. If you say so.'

Chapter Thirteen

'Lynn! There you are! Where have you been?'

'Just powdering my nose, love, like I told you. What you looking so upset about?'

'Oh, nothing. I guess I'm silly. I still seem to worry when you're out of my sight. And there's something about being in a hotel lounge that bothers me. It feels like the sort of place where a person might be left hanging around for the rest of his life, waiting and waiting for someone that doesn't come.'

'Now, *that's* not nice, Prof. Didn't I promise I wouldn't walk out on you?'

'Yes, you did. I'm sorry, Lynn. I'll be all right when we're in Scotland. I suppose I can't believe my luck, that's what it is. And you were away so long. At one time I was sure you'd gone out by another entrance. Another time I thought you were telephoning.'

'What?'

'Telephoning. I took a walk round the lobby, I couldn't sit still, and there was someone just leaving one of the phone-boxes that I thought was you. But she had her back to me, and she'd vanished round a corner before I got there.'

'Must have been somebody else, pet. I been powdering my nose, like I said. *Really* powdering my nose, as a matter of fact. We been living a bit rough these last two days, after all. It was time I took myself in hand. The toilets are lovely here, they got everything you could need. Here, Gray, you haven't told me how I look.'

'You look wonderful, Lynn. You look terrific.'

'Worth waiting for, eh?'

'Oh, yes, yes!'

'Well, then, let's go and eat. Here, take this, Gray, it's to pay the bill with.'

'It's too much, Lynn.'

'It's not, pet. It won't cost much less than that by the time we've finished. We're going to have a real good meal, and we're not going to hurry. We're celebrating, remember.'

'Yes, Lynn.'

'The happiest day of your life. That's what you said. So start looking happy again, Gray, like you were this morning. You *are* still happy, pet, aren't you?'

'Yes, Lynn.'

'Well, that's that, pet. Enjoyed your meal?'

'Yes, Lynn, thank you. Thank you very much. I must give you the change.'

'Don't be daft, Prof, I don't want it.'

'There wasn't much, as a matter of fact.'

'I didn't think there would be. Costs the earth to eat at a place like this nowadays.'

'Then why –?'

'Let's not talk about it. Just a little treat. Finished now. Graham, let's sit in this lounge a bit longer before we go out.'

'Why, Lynn?'

'Well. 'S nice and warm.'

'*Too* warm, I'd have said. And we seem to have been here for hours, what with the time we were here before we had our meal, and the time we were eating, and now . . .'

'Calm down, pet, you're getting nervy again.'

'It's a fine day outside, Lynn, even if it *is* beginning to feel like autumn. I don't mind a nip in the air when it's nice and clear. Why don't we *walk* back?'

'Brr.'

'To our own little place on the canal bank. And then we'll be lovely and warm, all by ourselves.'

'I'd like to sit here, Gray. I – I –'

'Lynn! Are you all right? Here, take my hanky.'

'It's nothing, pet. Don't take no notice. It just came over me. I can't help it. Do you know, there's times even now when I think of poor little Butch and I can't help crying. He was so pathetic at the end. He didn't know what had hit him.'

'Lynn, darling, cheer up. Smile. Look, *I'm* smiling.'

'Yes, Gray, you are, aren't you? . . . Poor little Butch.'

'Lynn! Who's that man crossing the lobby? The big fellow. I've seen him before.'

'Have you, pet?'

'He's coming this way. Lynn! Is is somebody after us? Had we better run?'

'Don't panic, Gray. It's only Sam Bell. There's nothing wrong, you'll soon see . . . Hullo, Sam, I'm glad you've come. Graham here was a bit restless, but I didn't want to tell him the good news till I'd actually seen you. In case it all fell through.'

'Good news?' Graham said. 'What good news, Lynn? And I *thought* I knew him. I *do* know him.'

' 'Course you know me, son,' said Sam Bell. 'We met in the caff. You tried to knock me out. Thought I was making a pass at Lynn. Remember?'

'I remember,' Graham said.

'Don't worry, lad. I don't bear no malice.'

'But what's going on? Lynn, what's going on? What's all this about good news?'

'There, now, pet. Sit down a minute, Sam, while I tell Graham all about it. It's like this, Gray. I told you a tiny white lie, see. When you thought you saw me telephoning, well, I guess you did see me telephoning. Because I remembered today that my old friend Sam lives in Cobchester and works out of Gertrude Street Depot. And goes up to Scotland sometimes. And I thought, what if old Sam's due to go up that way in the next day or two? He might be able to pick us up and save us a lot of bother. So I rang him. And what do you know, Gray. Sam *is* going up there. This very day. So that's the good news, pet. We got a ride.'

'Today's Sunday,' Graham said.

'You don't know much about transport, do you, love? Sam goes up today, empty, to pick up a load tomorrow morning. That's right, isn't it, Sam?'

'That's right, Lynn.'

'But Lynn, I still don't understand,' Graham said. 'Why didn't you *tell* me you were arranging all this?'

'It's like I said, love. I didn't want to disappoint you if it all fell through.'

'But we're supposed to be in this together. I can stand a disappointment. It wouldn't have mattered all that much.'

'Well. 'S not only that. It's with knowing you're a bit nervous, love, and with it being Sam of all people. I thought you might not like the idea. So I thought it'd be best if you met him face to face, so's you could be sure he didn't mean you no harm.'

'I told you, lad,' said Sam, 'I don't bear no malice.'

'I didn't know you and Lynn were such old friends.'

'We've known each other a long time, son. I

always come into Jeff's when I'm on the other run, going south. But don't get things wrong, there's never been anything between us. I'm married, you know. Mind you, I'll admit I envy you in a way . . .'

'He knows about us, Gray.'

'So I see.'

'But it's not my nature to be jealous,' said Sam.

'And where does Jeff come into this?'

'He doesn't, son. Jeff's no friend of mine. Last time I was there he practically threw me out. You ought to remember. If it wasn't that I don't bear malice, even to Jeff, you could say that I'm *for* anybody that Jeff's *against*. You pinched a girl from Jeff, and good luck to you, that's what I say. And if I can help you, I will. *Now* do you trust me, lad?'

'I suppose so.'

'Well, Sam,' said Lynn, 'where's the truck? You haven't parked it in front of the Royal Britannia, I suppose?'

'No, Lynn. I *would* have left it there, but the doorman didn't seem to fancy it. It's in a side-street.'

'Bring it round, Sam. Off you go, we'll see you in a minute . . . There you are, Gray, everything's fixed up. We'll be the only people this year to be collected from the main entrance of the Royal Britannia in a ten-ton truck.'

'Lynn. *Do* you trust him? Really?'

'Sam and me understand each other,' said Lynn.

'So it's good-bye to the old home,' Graham said.

'Yes, pet.'

'It's funny, although we've only been here such a short time I feel quite attached to it. We were happy here, last night and this morning. Weren't we, Lynn?'

'Yes, pet. Still, you wanted to be on your way,

didn't you? And we're going sooner than we expected.'

'It still feels a bit sad, leaving.'

'That's life, Gray. Where's Sam? Oh, he's been putting his overalls on. Hey, Sam, this way. Into the end cottage and up the ladder.'

Sam Bell stood in the middle of the attic.

'I don't think much of that bedstead,' he said. 'A real old relic. But the mattress doesn't look too bad.'

'It's lumpy,' said Graham.

'Well, you should know, lad. Still, me and the wife's furnishing a house. It'd be better than nothing for the spare bed. How can we get it out of here?'

'You don't want that old thing, Sam,' said Lynn.

'I reckon I do. Now, what came in must go out, eh? There must be a way.'

'It'd go through that door at the end and you could lower it to somebody outside,' said Lynn. 'But if it was me, I wouldn't waste my time.'

'You're not me, Lynn. And I got lots of room in the back of the truck. Here, son, you'll give me a hand, won't you?'

Graham said nothing.

'There's other things, too,' said Sam, 'that might come in handy. That chest of drawers, for instance. A bit battered, but when all's said and done it's still a chest of drawers. You don't get much for nothing these days. And the oil-stove. Is it working?'

'Yes.'

'Old-fashioned but it's a good stove. And that rug. There's nothing wrong with that. Come on, son, I'm giving *you* a helping hand, so you can help me. It won't take five minutes to strip this place of all that's worth having.'

'Don't look so upset, Prof, love,' said Lynn. 'It's only common sense after all. Sam's furnishing a house, like he said. It's an expensive time for him. He's glad of all he can get.'

'We're all glad of all we can get, aren't we?' said Sam.

'Look, Prof, we're going up in the world. Isn't it a smashing view? And heather already. How far are we from Bonnie Scotland, Sam?'

'About an hour's run, I'd say, at the rate we're going now.'

'An hour. That's not long, is it? Is it, Prof? An hour to the border.'

'We'll be there about dark, then,' Graham said.

'Should be. And we're not exactly racing along, are we? I reckon Young Whatsisname could move just about as fast on that horse of his. Don't you think so, Prof?'

'I dare say, Lynn.'

'And a lot more romantic than us, sitting here three-in-a-row in front of Sam's truck . . . You're not saying much, Prof, are you? Tired?'

'I suppose so.'

'I thought you'd have been all excited by now.'

'I feel sort of strange, Lynn. As if it had stopped being real. As if we were in one of those dreams where you go on and on and on and never get to where you're going. I'm glad I'm not in a dream . . . Lynn, you're crying again. Are you still thinking of Butch?'

'Sorry, pet. It came over me again, all of a sudden. I'm better now. Here, Gray, why don't you tell me some more about Young Thingummy?'

'Oh, there's a lot of it, Lynn. We did it at school once. I only know one or two bits of it.

O young Lochinvar is come out of the west.
Through all the wide Border his steed was the best.
So faithful in love, and so dauntless in war,
There never was knight like the young Lochinvar.'

'It's nice, isn't it, Gray? Can't you remember any more?'
'Sorry, Lynn. I can only think of one other line.

"They'll have fleet steeds that follow," quoth young
    Lochinvar.'

'Lynn! You've still got tears in your eyes. You're not crying for young Lochinvar now, are you? Cheer up, love, they didn't stop him. He got his girl . . . Hey, Mr Bell. Sam, I mean. Is something the matter?'
'It's nothing much, son. The engine's not pulling like it should on this slope. I just want to look under the bonnet while it's still light. I'm stopping in the lay-by here. You two can get out and stretch your legs.'

'I ought to be helping him, Lynn.'
'He'll ask you, pet, if he needs help. Don't bother him unless he does. Sam knows all about engines. He'll fix it.'
'It's taking him quite a while.'
'Don't *worry* so. It'll all be the same in the end.'
'It's getting dark, Lynn. I can only just see those hills ahead. Do you think they're in Scotland?'
'I shouldn't wonder, pet.'
'I wish we were safely there and married.'
'Gray. Here. I want to kiss you.'
'That was nice, Lynn.'

'I do love you, Gray. You'll always be Young
Lockindoor to me. Here, I'm going to kiss you
again.'

'That was a long one, wasn't it, Lynn? I forgot
where I was. I forgot everything but you.'

'Forget me as well now, pet.'

'Lynn! What do you mean?'

'Good-bye, Prof, love.'

'Lynn! What's the matter?'

'God bless.'

'Lynn! Where are you going? Lynn! Lynn!'

The dark blue Rover drew into the lay-by. Mr
Hollis stepped out. He put an arm through
Graham's. Sam Bell loomed out of the dusk and
stood at the boy's other side.

'Come on,' Mr Hollis said. 'Don't make a scene.
There's no point. It's all over now.'

Chapter Fourteen

'Graham,' said Mr Hollis.

'Yes.'

'You won't do anything silly, will you? Like opening the car door and jumping out?'

'No.'

'Promise me.'

'I won't do anything like that.'

'Good. I'm glad you have some sense. Now, we'll be on our way. We'll be home in about three hours, with luck. And listen, Graham. Your mother's been ill with worry, but I'm not going to throw that at you, and neither will she. I've got her to agree that there'll be no reproaches. You can tell us everything when the time comes. When you're ready.'

'There's nothing to tell. And never will be. You said yourself, it's all over. Isn't that enough?'

'Graham.'

'Yes.'

'Were you dozing?'

'No.'

'I had a word with the girl. While you were waiting with Mr Bell.'

'Waiting with Mr Bell. That's one way of putting it. He held me like a pair of handcuffs.'

'I'm sorry, Graham, but he couldn't risk letting you get away. As I was saying, I had a word with the girl. Lynn. And she told me that nothing happened.'

'What do you mean?'

'You know what I mean. You know exactly what I mean. Now, to be frank, Graham, it seems an unlikely tale to me. You're a young man, you weren't doing all this so you could gaze into her beautiful blue eyes. But that's what she says. And that's what I shall tell your mother. Right?'

'Tell her what you like.'

'The point is, Graham, that whether it's true or not – and I'm not asking you about it – it's what I want your mother to believe. And I don't want you to tell her otherwise.'

'Why not?'

'Because it would hurt her, and you've hurt her enough.'

'She put the ornaments away, with Lynn watching.'

'Never mind that now. If you can't be tactful out of consideration for your mother, you can be tactful as part of a bargain. No recriminations on *either* side. Nothing to make an awkward situation worse. Right?'

'I suppose so.'

'In one way we're all very fortunate. We told people you'd gone to your grandmother's for a few days. So far as I know, there's been nothing to make people gossip. Nobody knows anything about this escapade. So remember, that's where you've been – on a visit to your grandmother. Right?'

'All right. If that's what you say.'

'Graham.'

'Yes.'

'Cheer up, boy, it's not the end of the world.'

'It is for me.'

'Nonsense. An episode, that's all. It seemed important while it lasted – to us and I'm sure to you

– but it's ended happily, with nobody any the worse. Except that it's cost me a little money.'

'What do you mean?'

'I had to arrange to collect you, Graham. I didn't just happen to be passing. Perhaps you'd like to know how it was done.'

'No, I wouldn't.'

'I think you should, Graham. Unlike you, I prefer to bring things into the light of day. I'll tell you the whole story.'

'I don't want to hear it.'

'We hadn't really got anywhere in finding you until lunchtime today. And then I had a telephone call from Mr. Wright. Your friend's late employer. Who in turn had had a call from Lynn to say we could collect you at the Royal Britannia Hotel in Cobchester.'

'I'm not listening. I tell you I'm not listening.'

'But Mr Wright had his doubts whether the girl could keep you there long enough for us to get to Cobchester. And in any case there might have been a scene, which would attract attention. We wouldn't have wanted that. Are you listening *now*, Graham?'

'No.'

'However, he was in touch with this man Bell, who apparently will do anything for a few pounds, and arranged with him to take you to that lay-by, which is the first past the junction with the road from Crimley. And that was that. All that remained was for me to pick you up and pay. It cost me three hundred pounds altogether.'

'I didn't ask you to pay it.'

'I know you didn't. But I paid it all the same. A hundred for Mr Bell.'

'How nice for him. And the rest for Jeff, I suppose.'

'Oh no, Graham. Nothing for Mr Wright. I gathered he'd be quite satisfied if he retrieved the girl. He didn't expect to be paid as well. The other two hundred was for her.'

'What? She took money from you?'

'She did indeed. That's what I wanted you to know. She not only took the money, she said I was to *tell* you she'd taken the money. That's how much she cared about your feelings.'

'I don't believe it.'

'It's true. I'm afraid. She sold you, Graham. She sold you for two hundred pounds, cash down. I hope you feel you're worth it.'

— She's a whore.

— Shut up.

— Worse than a whore.

— Shut up.

— Worse, worse, worse than a whore.

— No. Not Lynn. No.

— A whore sells her body. That's nothing. *She* sold *you*.

— It was a lie. She never did.

— You think your father was lying?

— Yes.

— You think your father was lying?

— Yes. Yes.

— You think your father was lying?

— No. Oh Lynn, you couldn't, you didn't. You couldn't do that to me. I love you.

— You *did* love her. Or thought you did. You don't now.

— I do.

— She sold you. Two hundred pounds.

— She said she loved me. She was kind to me. Again and again.

– Like she was to Butch. But you were worth more. She wouldn't get two hundred pounds for a mongrel dog. Or she'd have sold him, too. You or a dog, no difference.

– I still love her.

– Two hundred pounds.

– Shut up.

– Sold to the only bidder. Going, going, gone. Two hundred pounds.

– Shut up.

– No arguing with the facts.

– Love's not about facts. Love's about people. I don't understand but I love her. She's good, I know she's good.

– Two hundred pounds.

– I'll love her till I die.

– You don't love her. You only thought you did. It wasn't real. You'll soon forget. All but one thing. She sold you. You won't forget that. She sold you. Two hundred pounds.

Chapter Fifteen

'Is it nice, Graham?'

'Yes, Mother.'

'Better than those school dinners?'

'Yes, Mother.'

'I feel sorry for the boys who come a long way and can't get home at midday. I do think boys need a good midday dinner when they're growing.'

'Yes, Mother.'

'I must say you're looking quite well these days. I worried about you for a while, after the – the event. You were so pale and peaky, I wondered if you'd ever get over it. Oh, Graham, how *could* you . . .?'

'Mother!'

'I know. We don't talk about it. At least, you don't talk about it with me. I sometimes think your father knows more than I do. Which reminds me, Graham, he rang this morning. He says, will you go round and see him this afternoon, after school?'

'What does he mean? I see him every day.'

'He meant at the office. He wants you to call at the office.'

'I wonder why. Did he sound cross?'

'No, not at all. He said there was something he wanted to discuss with you, that's all. He thought the office was the right place. He said it was time you got used to going to the office.'

'Your father will see you now, Mr Graham.'

Graham closed the door behind him.

'He called me "Mr Graham", Father. Old Benson called me "Mr Graham".'

'Yes. Do you mind?'

'No. It sounded funny, that's all.'

'It's old-fashioned. But then, Benson *is* old-fashioned. And he's waited seventeen years for the privilege of calling you that. So I'm glad you don't grudge him it.'

'It's all the same to me. I don't care what people call me.'

'It means something to him. You know, Graham, although they're such a small staff they're very loyal. And they'll serve you as they've served me, which is to say, very well. Not that I'm thinking of retiring for a long time yet.'

'I didn't think you were.'

'I don't like that cynical tone, Graham. I thought you were getting over that.'

'Sorry, Father.'

'All right, son, forget it. Now, let me give you a glass of sherry. Only the clients get that, as a rule. But I think you should have one, as a future partner. Provided you pass your exams, of course.'

'Of course.'

'You'll be wondering why I asked you to come here.'

'Yes.'

'Well, partly it's because I feel you should be getting better acquainted with us all. But mostly it's because I have something to discuss with you. It's in connection with your escapade of a few weeks ago.'

'I don't want to talk about it.'

'Neither do I, Graham. And I very nearly decided not to. I got something through the post last week, and I've been wondering ever since whether I ought to show you it. And after careful thought I feel that in honesty I must. Take a look at this, will you? An envelope addressed to me, with a London postmark. And inside it, two hundred pounds. No letter, nothing else at all. There, Graham, drink up your sherry. I was afraid this would startle you, and obviously it has. You know who it's from, of course?'

'Yes.'

'An interesting thing is this. It's the same money that I gave her. I took the numbers of the notes. It's a little habit of mine, especially in any transaction that's at all unusual. These are the twenty ten-pound notes that I handed to your friend Lynn in the lay-by, up there on the road to Scotland. Now, Graham, do you know anything about it?'

'No.'

'You haven't heard from her?'

'No.'

'Directly or indirectly? In any shape or form?'

'No.'

'I've been pondering this development all week, Graham, and I still don't know what to make of it. But I felt I had to tell you. I couldn't *not* tell you. It wouldn't be proper accounting, or fair to the girl.'

'She didn't sell me,' Graham said slowly. 'She didn't sell me after all. She gave me back.'

'Well, yes, I suppose that's the net result.'

'I'm stupid, I should have known. She never meant to keep your money. When you tried to give her money before, she wouldn't take it, would she? She said you didn't have to pay her to go away. She didn't care about money. But why did she take it in the first place? Why hand me back to you? Why?'

'Whatever the reason, Graham, I'll admit that I'm glad she's returned it. I like to feel that even a girl like that is not entirely bad.'

'Not entirely bad? You make me sick. Who are you to judge Lynn? She's worth a hundred of any of us!'

'Don't sound so bitter, Graham. I hope this isn't going to unsettle you, just when we were getting on so well together. Perhaps I shouldn't have told you after all.'

'Why did she do it? That's what I want to know. If only I could find her, and ask!'

'You won't find her now. And anyway, Graham, I think the moment has passed.'

'We'll see about that!'

'Alice!'

'What? Who is it?'

'Alice. It's me. Graham. You remember me?'

'Yes, I remember you. Didn't expect to see *you* again.'

'Where's Jeff?'

'Out.'

'Will he be long?'

'What's it to do with you?'

'I wanted a word with you, that's all.'

'With *me*? All right, come round the back. Here, have a cup of tea, it's fresh, it's not out of the urn. Jeff's just gone across the road, he'll be away for half an hour. What do you want, lad?'

'Alice, where's Lynn?'

'How should *I* know?'

'She's left?'

'Yes.'

'You haven't heard from her?'

'No.'

'When did she leave?'

'You ought to know that. She left the day you did.'

152

'What? You mean she hasn't been back?'

'No. Haven't had sight or sound of her.'

'But what about Jeff?'

'Jeff's all right. We got a new girl in the caff now. Sally. Long black hair. Jeff likes her better than he did Lynn. He's not fretting.'

'But . . . I thought Jeff went to fetch her back. From the road to Scotland.'

'Oh aye. So he did. Well, he *meant* to bring her back. But nothing came of it. When he got there, she'd crossed the road and thumbed a ride the other way. Vanished. Jeff gave Sam Bell a telling-off for letting her go, but as Sam said, there was nothing he could do about it, he wasn't her keeper. Not that Sam ever cared much for Jeff anyway.'

'So you don't know where Lynn is now?'

'I told you. No.'

'My father had a letter that seemed to have come from her. Postmarked London.'

'That's where she'll be, then, most likely. And up to no good, I dare say. A flighty piece, Lynn. Though mind you, I've come across worse. This Sally, for instance. The way she manages to get what she wants, you wouldn't believe. Why, only the other day . . .'

'Thanks for the tea, Alice.'

'That's all right, lad. Drop in any time if you feel like a chat. Jeff won't mind, so long as we're not too busy. Don't be afraid of him, he won't bother you, he's wrote Lynn off and that's that.'

'You think you'll ever hear from her, Alice?'

'No. 'Course not. Nor see her, neither. Don't kid yourself, Graham. When a girl like Lynn leaves a place like this, she leaves it for good. She's gone, like many before her. Into thin air.'

★

– Be rational. Be the accountant's son. Look at the facts. Work it all out. Reach a conclusion. Calmly. And to begin with, don't flatter yourself. On the spur of the moment it started. She'd had enough of Jeff. She went off with you. As a joke, almost. But when she stopped to think, what then? What had you to offer? Not much. A furnished flat somewhere, jobs for both of you. In three or four years' time, children. And never free again. Oh yes, you wanted to marry her. Fine. But why should *she* want to marry *you*?

– Keep reasoning, keep on reasoning. That's not all.

– No, that's not all. You admit you weren't much of a catch. But she could have just walked out. Why should she give you away, why weep? Why be thought a whore, worse than a whore? Why take two hundred pounds, and send it back weeks afterwards?

– Well, go on. Why?

– For your own good, clot, that's what it was. She knew what was best for you. She knew you wouldn't go home unless she handed you over. She knew you wouldn't stay there unless you thought the worst of her. That's why she took the money, and wanted you to know she'd taken it. The only way to stop you pulling the world down, round your parents' ears and yours.

'I do think sometimes. In a simple way.' That's what she said. Oh strange simplicity.

– Love, fool, love. She loved you, she said so. Not in the way you wanted, but she loved you. She loved you enough to betray you and take the blame. She kept the money till your life was back to normal. Till it was too late. Because it *is* too late. Admit it.

– She thought I was feeble, didn't she? She thought I hadn't the guts to be free. And maybe she was right. Or maybe she knew it wasn't my kind of freedom.

Oh, Lynn, you knew too much. But nothing's the same now, not even Hollis and Son. In nine days you changed everything. And you did love me, didn't you, Lynn? More than you ever loved anyone. Even Butch.

. . . He was walking on cliffs, somewhere on the south coast, somewhere remote and beautiful. A clear blue day, the seagulls wheeling and dipping. She came to him along the cliff path. 'Prof!' she called to him. 'Lynn!' he called back. 'Lynn! It's you at last. Lynn! Lynn! . . .'

— Come off it, boy. Put away childish things. Be realistic. She's gone, like many before her. Gone into thin air. Gone.

— I might see her again some time.

— You won't.

— I'll never marry anyone else.

— You will.

— All right, it's over now. The end of the day. Tomorrow is another. Settle down, don't *worry* so. Good-night, Prof, love. Good-night, Lynn, love. God bless.

Some other books you might enjoy

UNEASY MONEY
Robin F. Brancato

What would you do if you won a fortune? That's what happens when Mike Bronti buys a New Jersey lottery ticket to celebrate his eighteenth birthday. Suddenly, everything looks possible: gifts for his family, treats for his friends, a new car for himself – but things don't work out quite as Mike expects them to. A funny sensitive story about everyone's favourite fantasy.

THE TRICKSTERS
Margaret Mahy

The Hamiltons gather at their holiday house for their customary celebration of midsummer Christmas in New Zealand, but it is to be a Christmas they'll never forget. For the warm, chaotic family atmosphere is chilled by the unexpected arrival of three sinister brothers – the Tricksters.

THREE'S A CROWD
Jennifer Cole

How much fun can you have when your parents are away? No housework, no homework, a BIG party, and plenty of boys. Hey, who's throwing pizza around and where's Mollie disappeared to with that strange guy? (The first book in the *Sisters* trilogy.)

BREAKING GLASS
Brian Morse

When the Red Army drops its germ bomb on Leicester, the affected zone is sealed off permanently – with Darren and his sister Sally inside it. Immune to the disease which kills Sally, Darren must face alone the incomprehensible hatred of two of the few survivors trapped with him. And the haunting question is: why did Dad betray them?

THIN ICE
Marc Talbert

Since his father left, a lot of things have been bothering Martin. But his biggest problem is Mr Raven. It's bad enough having a teacher interfere with his own private life, but when he finds out Mr Raven is secretly seeing his *mother*, it's more than Martin can handle.

FLAMBARDS
K. M. Peyton

It's not easy for Christina to survive the harsh rule of her cruel and bitter Uncle Russell and the household he dominates with his passion for horses. Only her close friendship with her younger cousin, Will, and the groom, Dick, make life bearable – that and the freedom, pleasure and excitement when she learns to ride.

FACING UP
Robin F. Brancato

Dave and Jep are the closest of friends. They are opposites in character but that makes life more interesting and Dave doesn't even mind Jep's girlfiend Susan tagging along. But things change when Susan makes a play for Dave . . .

GIDEON AHOY!
William Mayne

Eva can't help remembering what Gideon was like when he was very young – before he was deaf, before he was ill. Now every morning she hears him give his strange, inarticulate morning shout and feels again the distance his brain damage has brought between them. And now Gideon is going to have a job – a real job in the outside world. How is he going to cope?